DOLLY
FICTION

Christmas
Carole

MARY FORREST

To
Charky

Happy Christmas
Fondest love
Mummy & Pappa
xoxo

GREENHOUSE
PUBLICATIONS

First published in 1989 by
Australian Consolidated Press
54 Park Street
Sydney NSW 2000
in association with
Dolly magazine
Australian Consolidated Press
54 Park Street
Sydney NSW 2000 Australia

© Greenhouse Publications 1989

Book design by Lynn Twelftree
Cover design by David Constable
Typeset by Trade Graphics Pty Ltd
Printed in Australia by Griffin Press

National Library of Australia
  Cataloguing-in-publication data:

  Forrest, Mary.
  Christmas Carole.

  ISBN 0 86436 307 9.

  I. Title. II. Title: Dolly. (Series: Dolly fiction).

  A823.3

Chapter 1

When Carole woke that morning, it took her a while to work out where she was. For one thing, her room was smaller than usual—smaller, but at the same time more bare and open. Where were the posters that covered her wall? Where was her old desk with its brass key and little wooden compartments? Where was the comfortable mess she was used to living in?

She sat bolt upright. For a moment, impossible theories tumbled about in her sleepy brain. She had been kidnapped for ransom. She'd been stolen by aliens. She'd changed places in her sleep with a girl from another time.

Then her eyes started to focus better and everything clicked into place. No, she hadn't moved into the world of one of her favourite videos. She was still herself, Carole Carmody, Year 12 student at Leland Ladies College, only daughter of Michelle and Roger Carmody.

Michelle and Roger Carmody. That was getting closer to the problem. Her parents had been fighting for a while. In fact, when Carole looked back, she could see that they hadn't really been getting on well for ages, but over the past year the arguments had been getting more frequent and more noticeable.

And last night she and her mum had moved out.

To make absolutely sure that she was right, Carole groped around beside the bed and found her contact lenses. After she'd blinked them into place, she examined the room again. Now she could see every detail, instead of general shapes and colours of things, and sure enough, she was in a small room full of cardboard boxes and nothing else—bare walls, uncurtained windows, an empty built-in wardrobe, a small table and a bed.

On the table an alarm clock was ticking away. Carole glanced at it and gasped. She hurtled out of bed and hunted frantically for her school uniform. (Luckily she seemed to have had the sense to hang it on a hook behind the door the night before.) Then she hesitated for a moment and pushed the door open.

The first thing she noticed was her schoolbag, standing near the door. Carole sighed with relief. She'd been a lot smarter than she remembered last night. But the truth was, she didn't remember much about the whole evening. It was basically a blank, from the moment when her dad had stared uncomfortably at the window and mumbled, 'Well, Carole, I suppose this is goodbye for the moment.'

So now she looked around the flat as if she was seeing it for the first time. There wasn't much to notice. The lounge room was basically a small space full of boxes just like her bedroom, and the kitchen was a narrow corridor crammed with cupboards and benches. Carole wondered sadly how her mum would manage in it. She was a great cook: it was one of the few ways in which she'd fitted into the role of wife to a successful business man.

Carole was opening the fridge and discovering it hadn't been plugged in, when the front door flew open. Her mum hurried in, carrying a bulging shopping bag.

'Oh rats,' she said, annoyed. 'You're up already. I wanted to give you breakfast in bed.'

'I'm late enough already, Mish,' Carole protested. 'I didn't even have a shower, to make sure I got to school on time.'

'Well you won't catch a lingering disease, just because you missed one shower. But I thought you'd stay home today. I mean—well, after yesterday and everything … I just thought you might like to skip school for once.'

Carole looked down at her hands. It'd never occurred to her that she mightn't be going to school. That was her dad's influence, of course—he was the one who had always insisted on taking her temperature when she was a little kid, to check that she was really sick. Mish, on the other hand, didn't worry about things like showers and neatly ironed clothes and never missing a day of school.

Even her mum's name was a sign of the differences between her parents. Carole had always called her dad 'Dad'—it was only when she had to fill out forms for school that she ever thought of him as 'Roger'. But her mum had been 'Mish' since the day that Carole had learned to talk. It was short for 'Michelle', of course, but somehow it seemed to sum up her mum's friendly, easy-going personality.

'Listen, Mish, I'm happy to stick around if you need a hand with getting this place in order,' Carole said now. 'I was only planning to go to school because ... because it would make things seem more normal.'

'Well that makes a lot of sense,' Mish said brightly. 'I tell you what, I'll drive you there in the ute. I know you're more organised than me, but I bet you haven't worked out which buses will get you to Leland yet, and besides, it'll give you time for this great breakfast I've bought.'

She started to unpack with a flourish, holding up a bag of croissants, strawberry jam and cream. Her short, golden hair fluffed out around her head and, in her baggy windcheater and patched jeans, she looked more like Carole's big sister than her mum.

Mind you, it helps that I look older than I am, as well, Carole thought wryly. She'd got her height from her dad, along with her serious way of approaching the world, and Mish's curly head barely came up to Carole's chin.

Not only was she tall, she was solidly-built where Mish was fragile and delicate. So everyone was always telling her how sensible and reliable she was, even on days when she felt she was obviously looking for a shoulder to cry on. But it was too hard for her to find a shoulder at the right height, so by now Carole had given up trying.

'And look, they even had coffee beans in the corner shop, although they're not our usual sort,' Mish prattled on. 'I think we'll be able to manage very comfortably here ... won't we?'

There was a strained tone in her voice and Carole suddenly realised that Mish was doing her best to cheer them both up.

'Yeah, you've turned on a great breakfast,' she said hastily. 'I'm really looking forward to exploring this area.' They munched their way through two croissants each, telling each other between mouthfuls how good they were. Halfway through her last bite, Carole felt as though her throat was going to close over with misery, but a hurried swig of coffee solved that problem. She smiled across at Mish.

'Okay, it's time for you to get out the ute so I can drive to school in style,' she said jokingly.

Everything seemed to remind her of the problems between her mum and dad that morning. The ute had been another of the trouble zones. Her dad had always taken the train to work so, theoretically, the Volvo was free for Mish to use during the day, except that she insisted on driving everywhere in the old ute.

Her dad had been totally infuriated by this. 'We've got a good car, so why don't you use it?' he would say. 'You don't need to carry on as though you were still a hippy or something. What are people going to think?'

'How would I know?' asked Mish, genuinely puzzled. 'It takes me ages to work out what I think, most of the time. I know why I like the ute, though. I feel safe in it, whereas I always feel like I'm going to put a dent in the Volvo somewhere.'

'All right, I'll sell the ute,' Dad would roar. 'Then you'll be forced to take the Volvo.'

But he never carried out his threats, because they needed the ute when they went for weekends at the house in the country. As she settled into the front seat, tucking her schoolbag under her feet, Carole gulped suddenly, realising that she wouldn't be going to the house any more. Well, maybe she would, when she went to stay with Dad ... but it wouldn't be the same.

There were so many things to take in. Maybe Mish was right and she ought to stay home and have a bit of a think. No, it still didn't seem like a great idea. Better to let it all sink in, one thing at a time, than to hang around the flat, brooding about everything.

They made good time through the unfamiliar suburbs. Mish was a very competent driver. (Though she *had* put a dent in the Volvo, Carole remembered, the day her dad had bullied her into taking it out. Carole had always felt she'd done it 'accidentally on purpose'.) Before long, they caught sight of the string of Leland girls in their brown uniforms, walking down the hill towards the College from the bus stop.

Carole glanced down at her watch. 'Hey, we're early. I might get out here and stretch my legs before we're shut into those classrooms again.'

'Suits me,' Mish agreed. 'If I drop you off here, I can go straight on to the shops and stock up on provisions. Any special orders?'

'Just remember to get my usual breakfast cereal. Oh, and maybe we could have egg and bacon pie tonight.'

That was the traditional Sunday night supper from her childhood, though she couldn't remember Mish making it for years. Even thinking about it made Carole feel more secure inside, and from the warm look her mum gave her, Mish understood too.

'Eggy bacon pie it is,' she said with a grin, using Carole's childish name for the treat. 'Do you want me to pick you up tonight, or can you find your way back?'

'I'll be fine,' Carole said firmly, swinging herself out of the car. 'See you later.'

She strode down the hill, pretending to herself that she'd arrived by bus as usual. As she walked in the gates, her best friend, Giovanna Corelli, hurried up behind her.

'Boy you've got long legs,' she complained.

'I've been chasing you all the way down the hill, ever since I saw your mum letting you out of the car.'

'Oh right, I slept in this morning,' Carole said instantly. 'Mish had to give me a lift, so I wouldn't be late.'

'Carole Carmody late for school,' Giovanna marvelled. 'What next?'

Chapter 2

So evidently she didn't plan to tell her best friend about the most important change in her life, even though, ever since she'd come to Leland Ladies College, Carole had been in the habit of telling Gee everything.

Gee. How come all the people in her life had these jazzy nicknames? Mish-short-for-Michelle. Gee-short-for-Giovanna. Even her boyfriend was Drew-short-for-Andrew, instead of being called something more ordinary like Andy. As for herself, no one ever called her Caz or Carrie or anything like that. She wasn't jazzy enough for a jazzy nickname.

Carole spent the rest of the morning trying to think of a nickname that would change her image. It was better than thinking about her parents. It was even better than thinking about why she hadn't told Gee that her parents had split up.

But at lunchtime, she had to go a step further. Up till now, she'd simply said nothing to Gee about home. But as they opened their lunches, Gee said casually, 'So how are things?' and Carole had to make up her mind in a split second.

Normal, she thought desperately. I came to school because I wanted it to be a normal day. You normally don't have everyone fussing over you.

So she took a big bite of her croissant with vegemite—which was all they'd had in the house—and said indistinctly, 'Fine. How about you?'

Gee was in love, of course. She specialised in love—she'd often said she wished she could take it as a school subject, because then at least she'd be sure of one reasonable mark. She'd fallen in love with guys at the opposite end of the disco. She'd fallen in love with guys on pushbikes when she spotted them from the bus window. And her personal best was falling in love with a guy when all she could see were his legs sticking out from under the car he was mending.

Strangely enough, Gee just about always ended up talking to the guys and going out with them. Even more strangely, they all turned out to be real hunks. Not that it did them any good, since Gee got tired of the guys as fast as she fell in love with them.

'I don't quite know how it happens,' she confessed to Carole. 'I meet this guy and I think he's really terrific, so we fall in love and

14

it's happy-ever-after time—until I meet another terrific guy.'

Fortunately Gee managed the whole business so cheerfully that the guys never held a grudge. And Gee's friends benefitted, because she tried to pass the guys on to them on the basis that, since she was still fond of them, she wanted them to be happy. That was how Carole had first met up with Drew. (He'd been the guy on the pushbike, and Carole had actually seen him first, though of course it was Gee who'd started a conversation with him. Carole was still grateful to her for that—left to herself, she might never have said hello to Drew, and now they'd been going out together for six months.)

At any rate, this time Gee was sure she'd found a guy she really wanted to spend a lot of time with. 'I mean, Sean's good-looking,' she told Carole, 'but looks don't really matter to me. We've got the same sense of humor, though, and that's a big attraction.'

'If looks don't matter to you, then how come all the guys you go out with are totally gorgeous?'

Gee looked genuinely puzzled. 'Yeah, I've often wondered about that myself. Haven't come up with an answer, yet, though.'

Carole laughed. Sometimes she was tempted to feel jealous of her friend, but basically it never lasted for long. Gee was beautiful, with her rich black curls, dark long-lashed eyes and rounded figure, and Carole always felt pretty washed-out beside her. At the same time, Gee was also incredibly kind and generous, as well as being unconcerned about her own looks, so Carole had decided that jealousy was really a waste of time.

'So are you seeing Drew this Friday?' Gee went on. 'I'm trying to work out whether this week's a girls' night out or not, so I can settle my plan of action with Sean.'

Gee and Carole, along with a group of their friends, had been going to the same disco, Anticipation, on Friday night for the past couple of years, and over time they'd developed a tradition in which sometimes the girls brought their boyfriends of the moment and sometimes they planned a girls' night out. Carole usually knew she'd enjoy herself on a Friday night, whatever else happened during the rest of the week, but this time the mention of Drew's name made her bite her lip thoughtfully.

Though Drew and she generally only saw each other at the weekend, they often rang each other up during the week to exchange news or consult about their homework or just to keep in touch. But if Drew rang Carole's house, her dad would tell him that she didn't live there any more, and then her secret would be out.

She'd have to ring Drew as soon as she got home, before he could possibly have rung her. And she'd have to think up some brilliant reason why he couldn't ring her at home in the future, which wouldn't be easy. Maybe she could ask her dad to say she was in the shower and that she could ring back. Then he could ring her and tell her to ring Drew and—no, it was much too complicated, and besides, her dad was more likely to say something cutting than to agree. She'd just have to think up some other plan on the way home.

Life was becoming incredibly difficult. Carole sighed and Gee looked at her with concern. 'Are you sure you're okay?' she asked. 'You look really pale—you could be catching flu or something.'

'I told you before, I'm fine,' Carole snapped.

Then she suddenly saw the funny side of it. She was angry at Gee for not believing her—but actually she was lying to Gee, so she didn't deserve to be believed. She giggled quietly and Gee smiled back with relief.

'That's better. Now, let me tell you some more about Sean.'

Carole was happy to sit back and listen to Gee. She was happy to sit back and listen to her teachers raving on about history and maths. It was all a way of putting off the problems she'd have to face later on.

To begin with, she and Gee usually walked up to the bus stop together, though luckily they caught different buses. If she was going to continue pretending that nothing had changed, she could hardly admit to Gee that she ought to be heading in the opposite direction. Still, hopefully Gee's bus would come first, and then Carole could set off to the other side of the road.

The moment they got to the top of the hill,

a bus trundled along. Carole was still trying to check its number when Gee gave her a push.

'That's your bus, dillbrain. If you run you'll just catch it.'

Carole did her best to miss the bus. She jogged as slowly as possible and, when that wasn't working, she dropped her bag and stopped to pick it up. Normally the driver would've given her a sadistic grin and revved away, but this time, of course, the woman kindly kept the doors open and waited for her.

Carole fumbled for her student pass with one hand and waved to Gee with the other. 'Thanks,' she gasped to the bus driver, then added, 'for nothing' under her breath. She wriggled between the passengers until she reached the crowd around the door. When the bus stopped further down the street, she slipped off as secretly as possible, so the driver wouldn't notice and regret her good deed.

Once she was out in the street again, she was hit by another problem. Gee's bus came down this stretch of road too, and Gee would think it was pretty weird if she noticed her standing on the opposite footpath. Carole crossed the road and looked around. The bus stop was outside a church, and in front of the church there was a large noticeboard with a Bible text on it.

Carole hesitated and then ducked behind the noticeboard. After all, people had hidden in churches in the olden days when they wanted to escape from trouble, hadn't they? She kept peering nervously around the edge of the board and when a bus appeared, she waited till the last minute before leaping out to hail it.

As the bus roared off, she glanced back and read the Bible text for the first time. *'Be sure your sins will find you out,'* it said in tall white letters. Carole fidgeted uncomfortably. It didn't seem like a good omen. But here she was on the homeward bus, so no one was really likely to find out she'd been lying her head off all day, were they?

After a while she managed to get a seat at the back of the bus, which made it easier to check the route. To Carole's alarm, the streets suddenly looked quite different from the ones Mish had driven along this morning. Grabbing hold of her bag, she went down to the front of the bus again and asked the driver whether he went through her suburb.

He frowned for a moment and Carole had a horrible feeling that she was lost in her own city. Then he repeated the name of the suburb in a strong Vietnamese accent, and she realised he must've found her pronunciation hard to understand.

'Yes, of course,' he said. 'You must get off at High Street and catch another bus.'

'Um, where's High Street?' Carole asked in a small voice.

'We pass High Street three stops ago.'

'Oh. Thank you.'

So maybe she wasn't doing so well after all. As

Carole trudged back along the road, the evening wind began to blow coldly around her legs, and the darkening sky seemed a pretty accurate reflection of her mood. Then the light of a phone box gleamed out at her. For a brief moment she struggled with her desire to be independent and self-reliant, before she pulled out her diary, found the phone number of the flat and rang Mish.

'I knew it was a lucky sign that I could get the phone connected before we moved in,' Mish enthused as Carole clambered into the ute. 'And honestly, you wouldn't believe how much better the place looks, now I've cleared away most of the boxes. I think we made the right choice.'

For once Mish wasn't exaggerating. When Carole walked in, she could barely recognise the unwelcoming room she'd left that morning. Mish's treasures were spread around on the bookshelves and small tables. Brightly-coloured cushions had been piled on the floor to take the place of a couch. There were pictures on the wall, and makeshift curtains covered the venetian blinds.

'Of course things will improve after I really get to work on finding furniture and stuff,' Mish said earnestly. 'Still, it's not bad, is it?'

She had her pleading look on again, but this time Carole was able to say sincerely, 'It's fantastic, Mish. I don't know anyone else who could have done so much in such a short space of time.'

Mish looked pleased. 'All right, now you can go and have the shower you missed this morning. Your fingers are like ice—you need to warm up. And while you're getting ready, I'll finish the dinner.'

After all the experiences Carole had had that day, it was wonderful to lounge on the cushions in her dressing gown, eating egg and bacon pie with her fingers and watching the latest drama series on the old TV that they used to keep in the sun room. The reception wasn't too good and Mish kept assuring her it'd improve once she worked out how to connect the TV to the building's aerial, but Carole didn't care. For the first time in ages, she felt warm and secure and almost happy.

So it was with an unpleasant jolt she remembered she had to ring Drew. Before she could chicken out, she heaved herself up from the cushions, found the phone and dialled his number.

'Great, I was just about to ring you,' he said cheerfully. 'I need you to explain the parliamentary system to me again.'

Carole opened her mouth and then shut it again. There was no point in saying, 'But I haven't unpacked those books yet,' not unless she wanted to let Drew in on her secret. Decisions, decisions, she sighed, wondering what was the best thing to do.

Then she found herself saying, 'Actually that's why I was ringing you. I've got a lot of work to do for school this week, so I really have to cut down on phone calls. I can tell you about parliament first, of course, but...'

'Don't bother,' Drew said more coolly. 'I can probably figure it out for myself. Are you still going out with me on Friday, or are you cutting down on discos too?'

'No, that'll be good,' Carole said miserably.

Drew hung up as soon as they'd arranged to meet, and Carole stood and stared at the receiver. Maybe that sign outside the church had been right after all. She hadn't been caught out in her lies, but she'd landed herself in as much trouble as she had dodged.

Chapter 3

It had been hard to settle down and do the minimum amount of homework she could get away with. It had been hard to find the street directory and work out her route to school. It had been hard to forget the sound of Drew's cool voice.

But it was shockingly easy to cry herself to sleep.

As a result, Carole woke next morning feeling as though the night had made her more tired, instead of rested. She held the alarm clock to her nose and squinted at it in disbelief. Then she remembered her plan and dragged herself out of bed, groaning softly.

She was slapping a hasty sandwich together when Mish appeared beside her. 'Carole, it's incredibly early,' she said sleepily. 'Do you need to get up this early to go to school?'

Carole was about to say 'Yes,' but just in time she realised that, if she did, Mish would get upset and decide she'd chosen a flat in the wrong area, after all.

'Didn't I tell you?' she said brightly. 'We've got singing practice before school, all this week. Don't worry, you can still sleep in.'

'Thanks, I will,' Mish croaked and tottered back to bed.

Carole let herself out into the grey morning, clutching the sheet of paper with her directions written on it. Another lie, she thought gloomily. She was going to trip herself up on her own stories soon, if she wasn't careful. The truth was, she wasn't cut out for this sort of thing, but she'd started the whole business and now she had to keep on with it.

This morning she'd have to catch a total of three buses, in order to meet Gee at the top of the hill. Of course she could always have walked down the road and caught the train to Leland Ladies College, which would've got her there in less than half the time. Mish hadn't made a mistake in the location of the flat—it was just that if Carole went to school by train, she'd have to walk up the hill instead of down it. And then Gee would want to know what was going on.

Of course, Mish would want to know what was going on, too, if she kept getting up early next week. Drew would want to know what was going on too if she told him not to ring her next week as well. With all her lies, she'd really only brought herself one week of peace and quiet.

Then again, anything could happen in a week.

Only last week, she'd been living comfortably in her dad's house, with a huge bedroom, her own bathroom, an enormous TV to watch and every luxury that money could provide—a pretty different life to the one she was leading now. So she could hang in there for a week, maybe things would change for the better again.

But, by Friday nothing much had changed at all, except that Carole was totally exhausted. This meant that she had no energy to waste worrying about her parents or Drew, but that was the only advantage. She was falling behind in her school work, for the first time that she could remember, and although she was putting in a lot of effort to meet up with Gee, when they actually got together Carole was too tired to have anything to say.

As Carole sat in class and watched her favourite teacher draw a historical time line on the board, she was alarmed to notice that the chalk lines seemed to be growing fuzzy and melting into their black surroundings. She blinked hastily, feeling a surge of panic. What if her eyesight was getting worse again?

But as soon as she made an effort, the writing came into focus, and Carole realised it was just another symptom of being tired out. She would've liked to put her head down on the desk and go straight to sleep, except she had a feeling it'd be a bad move. Next minute Gee nudged her in the ribs, and finally it sank in that the teacher had been calling her name.

'Well, Carole, I've actually got your attention at last,' she commented. 'Do you want to make a guess at which should come next on the time line—the Rum Rebellion or the Eureka Stockade? Or haven't you been listening to this lesson at all?'

Carole could see that, under her sharp manner, the history teacher was still being kind to her. She'd given her a choice of possibilities, so Carole could make a guess and have a fifty per cent chance of being right. She knew that's what she was supposed to do—she knew no one ever openly admitted they hadn't been listening to a teacher.

All of a sudden, though, she was tired of telling lies. 'I wasn't listening,' she said flatly.

Just as she expected, the history teacher looked taken aback. 'Well, that's either very rude or very honest,' she said. 'Which is it, Carole?'

More questions, Carole thought despairingly. If she answered this time, the teacher would only ask her another. Not that she could answer, because she didn't have a clue what to say, even though she hated to let her favourite teacher down.

So instead she burst into tears. There was a brief silence and then the teacher said, with unexpected sympathy in her voice, 'Gee, why don't you take Carole out into the garden for the rest of this period, to give her a chance to recover?'

Carole stumbled to her feet. Gee's hand was at

her elbow, guiding her down the aisles of desks, through corridors lined with lockers, and along the stone path which led to the garden at the front of the school.

'Come on, tell me about it,' Gee said softly.

Carole kept on staring at the shifting patterns of green leaves overhead. 'What do you mean?' she said defensively.

'Oh well, I hoped you were going to tell me yourself, but since you're determined to do an imitation of a clam, I might as well say straight out that I know what's been happening.'

Carole wondered briefly whether she could still pretend that she didn't understand, but she decided this would be pushing it. 'How did you find out?' she demanded.

'You seemed a bit strange on Monday, so I rang you as soon as I got home. Your dad answered and told me that you and your mum had moved out. He sounded pretty surprised that you hadn't told me, but don't worry—I pretended I knew already and that I'd just dialled your old number automatically.'

'Thanks,' Carole said awkwardly. She felt deeply grateful to Gee. If Mish found out what she'd been doing, she'd probably just laugh or give her a hug, but her dad was a matter of fact kind of person who'd think she was off her rocker for trying to mislead everyone.

'Mind you, I only pretended I knew already. I still haven't heard the full story,' Gee prompted.

'Oh, right.' Carole took a deep breath and

began. 'Well, Mish and Dad have been fighting for so long that I really didn't take much notice of it. I mean, some people enjoy it, right?'

'Right,' Gee agreed fervently. Gee's aunt and uncle were definitely in that category, and most of their big family dinners were enlivened by a screaming match at some stage in the process.

Carole grinned, remembering some of Gee's stories. 'But your aunt and uncle enjoy making up, too, and that's what was missing between Mish and Dad. I'd been feeling kind of relieved lately, because they'd stopped sniping at each other over dinner, and generally they seemed to be making a big effort to get on better together.'

'Oh yeah?' Gee said in surprise. 'Then how come they split all of a sudden?'

'It *was* sudden,' Carole said, remembering. 'Dad came home one day and said he was going to America on a business trip. He was pretty pleased—he's never been to America, and it was a sign that his firm was likely to promote him. But Mish started screaming at him that this was just another example of him putting his business before his family life. She said they'd agreed to spend six months trying to make their marriage work and she'd been doing her best, but if he wasn't going to do his share, then she didn't see why she should bother.'

Gee's eyes opened wide. 'I've never seen Mish in a rage. She always seems to be so relaxed and cheerful.'

'She certainly wasn't relaxed the other night,'

Carole said with a watery grin. 'Dad terrified me even more, though, because he went all cold and controlled. He said' (she shut her eyes, recalling his exact words), 'In that case, we might as well put an end to this experiment. We're not suited to each other any more, Michelle, and there's no point pretending we are.'

'He called her Michelle?' Gee asked in an awed voice.

Carole nodded hard. 'That's when I knew it was really serious. He's always tried to stop me calling her Mish, because he reckoned it wasn't dignified. But he used the name Mish himself, all the same, just like all her friends do. It was as if he was suddenly turning her into a different person.'

'His ex-wife, instead of his wife,' Gee said cynically. Carole shivered and Gee reached over to pat her shoulder. 'I'm sorry, I shouldn't be making jokes about it. How did you feel while all this was going on?'

'I felt like I wanted to hide under the table,' Carole said. 'The worst part hadn't even started, though. They went straight into discussing how they'd separate. Dad said they ought to wait till he went overseas, since it was only a few weeks, but Mish said that was a few weeks too many. She reckoned she'd find a flat and move into it over the weekend. Then they both turned and looked at me.'

'Freaky,' Gee breathed. 'I bet you really wanted to hide under the table then.'

'I reckon! I thought they might both grab one of my arms and try to pull me into two. But instead Dad said politely, "I suppose you'd prefer to live with your mother, Carole," and Mish said, "Your father can offer you more advantages, you know".'

Her eyes filled with tears and she turned her head away as the memory of that moment swept over her. Beside her, she could hear Gee saying indignantly, 'So they tried to rip you in two, after all,' and she swung around again, forgetting to hide the tears.

'What do you mean?'

'Well, they were forcing you to choose, weren't they? I mean, there are all kinds of different arrangements for kids of divorced parents these days—it's not a question of siding with one parent or other.' Carole started to protest and Gee continued energetically, 'Oh, I know they weren't openly asking you to take sides, but that's what makes me maddest. They were pretending to be fair, except that really they were both trying to get their own way.' When Carole still looked doubtful, she added, 'It's like when you go, "Oh, please have the last piece of cake", in order to force the other person into being polite and giving it to you.'

Carole stared away across the garden, thinking about what Gee had said. A hard knot of misery in her stomach seemed to be dissolving as she sat there. It was true, she'd felt that she had to choose between her parents, and basically she'd felt she'd let them both down. That was why she'd wanted to pretend that the whole thing had never happened.

But if Gee was right, then her parents had contributed by putting her in a false position. It was strange—she knew Mish and her dad were human beings who could make mistakes, just like anyone else. At the first sign of trouble, though, she'd retreated to the ideas she'd had as a little kid, when her parents could do no wrong and she was the one who was often naughty.

With a sigh of relief, Carole decided that Mish and her dad were still human beings after all, in which case the three of them were all muddling along as well as they could in a difficult situation. She liked that way of thinking about things. It made her feel as though, in some ways, the three of them continued to be linked together, even if life could never be the same as it was before.

'Thanks, Gee,' she said gratefully. 'Talking to you has helped heaps.'

Chapter 4

It was a relief to discover that she'd been thinking she was the one at fault. At the same time, however, Carole felt a bit silly for having gone to all that effort to hide something she'd never really had a chance of hiding.

'Well, I hope that's the end of all those singing practices,' Mish said to her when she arrived home. 'It's a terrible thing to do to you, so close to the exams. If it was continuing on, I'd write to the school about it.'

Carole was glad she'd already sorted things out with Gee, because otherwise she would've been in even more trouble. For a moment she was tempted to tell Mish the real story. Then she remembered Mish had her own problems. There was no point in getting her worried, especially when that particular episode was well and truly over.

On the other hand she definitely needed to

give Drew some explanations, after handing him that feeble story about the phone calls. All the way to the city, Carole planned how she was going to do it. She'd tell him the truth, of course—the whole truth, too, so that there wouldn't be any more misunderstanding. But she'd do it casually, with a joke or two maybe, to make it clear she was coping okay.

After this sensible decision, she caught sight of Drew in the city square, rushed over to him and babbled, 'Oh Drew, Mish and Dad have split up. I'm living in a flat with Mish and that's why I told you not to ring me at home. I've sorted it all out, though, and I'm feeling much better.'

Then she burst into tears.

Drew patted her shoulder for a while and finally presented her with a clean hanky. As she scrubbed away the tears, he said, 'That's tough. But don't take it too seriously, Carole. Half the kids in my class spend their time shuttling between two parents. You'll get used to it.'

'I suppose I will,' Carole said in a small voice, returning the hanky. She would've liked to go on talking about it but, after what Drew had said, there didn't seem to be anything more to add. Of course she'd get used to it. You could probably get used to anything—being a paraplegic, say, or an orphan or …

Stop being morbid, she told herself quickly. She pulled herself together and asked Drew to repeat what he'd just said.

'I was just suggesting that we have dinner at

the new sushi bar before we go to the disco,' he said patiently. 'How does that sound to you?'

Carole had been to Japanese restaurants with Drew before. She liked the food—she'd even come to appreciate the taste of the raw fish in the sushi—but she knew that the prices weren't on the cheap end of the scale.

'I'm not all that hungry,' she murmured. 'Maybe we could just have a salad and a coffee at the Diner Inn.'

'Sushi isn't that filling. Besides, I'm happy to eat half of your serve,' Drew said, grinning.

When Drew set his mind on something, he generally got his way. Carole decided it was better to give in gracefully. She could always order a small serve.

'There, I knew we'd given the right order,' Drew said later with a smile. 'You'd never have made it through the evening on one small salad.'

Carole forced a smile in return. For a moment after she'd seen the bill, she'd had some doubts about whether she was going to make it through the evening on the money left in her purse. Luckily, there was just enough to pay for the disco and the train home—but what was she going to do after that?

It seemed like she had just got rid of one problem and another sprang up to hit her in the face. So far she'd been concentrating on the difficult feelings around her parents' separation, but there were other more practical problems as well—like money, for example.

She'd complained silently about having to leave her luxurious home and live in a pokey little flat, but she hadn't realised that this would carry over to her day to day living. What would happen about her allowance? Mish hadn't mentioned it and Carole didn't like to ask. Mish had made a big deal about not taking any expensive furniture—the only good pieces in the flat were the ones Mish had restored herself, like Carole's desk. So Carole couldn't imagine that Mish had accepted much money from her dad—if any.

What about her, though? Her fees at Leland Ladies College had been paid already—both her parents had explained carefully that the separation wouldn't affect her schooling. Her dad must've paid the fees, so was he also supposed to pay something towards her food and clothing and things like that? She would've liked to ask Drew what had happened with the kids in his class, but she couldn't do that without bringing up her money worries, and somehow she didn't feel comfortable about that.

Drew tapped the bill with slight impatience and Carole hastily handed over a twenty dollar note. She watched it go regretfully. She'd never needed to worry about money before. Though her dad was pretty strict in some ways, he'd always been happy to give her something extra if she went over her allowance or saw some terrific piece of clothing she simply had to own.

Well, she'd just have to do a crash course in

budgeting, starting from now.

'Okay, let's go,' Drew announced. 'We'll be a bit early, but who cares? I've got dancing feet tonight, and it won't bother me if we're the only ones on the floor.'

For the next few blocks Drew proved to her that he had been telling the truth. He raced her from one corner to the next, caught her up and whirled her round, then waltzed her over to a lighted window to admire a fancy striped waistcoat.

'How would I look in that?' he demanded. 'Here, there's one on the female model too. We could be twins and stun everybody at the disco.'

Carole had been laughing along with him, but suddenly the smile was wiped from her face. 'I ... I don't look too good in waistcoats,' she stammered.

'Spoilsport,' Drew said, but he was smiling and she heaved a sigh of relief. All the same, she could see another set of problems on the way. How would Drew take it when she couldn't afford to give in gracefully to his more expensive ideas?

Well, she'd just have to cross that bridge when she came to it. Right now, she only had to cross the road to queue in front of Anticipation. As Drew had said, they'd arrived early, so the queue was still short. Within minutes they were inside and Drew's eyes were lighting up at the sight of an almost empty dance floor.

'Here's when I get my chance to show off all the things I learned in dancing class,' he exclaimed. 'I've often wondered why my parents bothered to send me along. When you've got a tiny square to dance on there's no point in knowing how to do the tango or the rumba. I always thought they were punishing me—you know, "we went to dancing class, so you've got to go to dancing class." But for once I can really have a whirl with you.'

Carole felt a bit nervous at first. She'd never had any interest in dancing classes, and 'tango' and 'rumba' just sounded like the names of icecreams to her. Drew was an excellent dancer, though. And Carole had a good sense of rhythm, so she found she could anticipate his moves and blend in with them.

Several people actually clapped them at the end of a particularly spectacular turn. 'That's all very well,' Drew grumbled, 'but you can't really demonstrate the tango to a disco beat. This just isn't the right kind of music.'

He tapped his foot irritably, waiting for the next track, but instead the DJ's voice crackled from the microphone. 'Well done to the tango twosome,' he said. 'Yep, I know the dance myself, and I found a track at the bottom of the stack that'll set your heels clicking. It's an old favourite, and I mean *old*. Out of the dark ages, also known as the fifties, comes the biggest tango of them all. So clear the floor for the tango twosome and Hernando's Hideaway.'

Something was wrong but Carole didn't have time to think about what it was. To her surprise, the other dancers really were leaving the floor and Drew was straightening his back and holding out his arms.

This is ridiculous, Carole thought in a panic. Five minutes ago I thought 'tango' was an icecream flavour, and now I'm supposed to demonstrate it to the whole disco. She didn't have time to back out, though, because the first guitar notes were already sounding.

Drew had been right. The music did make a difference. With Drew and the rhythm to help her, Carole found herself adding her own flourishes to the basic steps. She flicked her skirt out on the turns, she allowed herself to go limp in Drew's arms as he bent her this way and that. They were getting into the romance of the movements and sending them up at the same time, so that Carole was suddenly reminded of why she'd been attracted to Drew in the first place.

Which was weird, because she hadn't noticed that he'd lost any of his attraction for her.

Drew flung her backwards as the last chord sounded and she bent in a graceful arc in his arms. The applause was even louder than before. Drew swung her upright and they bowed to the crowd, grinning broadly.

'Who needs dancing lessons? You're doing fine without them,' Drew complimented her. 'Come on, I want to say thanks to the new DJ.'

The new DJ. That's what was wrong. From where she stood, Carole hadn't been able to see him properly, but she'd known that the voice wasn't right.

While Drew raved on about Hernando's Hideaway, Carole scowled at the new DJ. He couldn't be described as the glamorous type—he was tall and skinny, with a beaky nose and a tangle of red curls that flopped down over his forehead. Nothing like the neat dark little DJ who'd spun the discs for all the years that Carole had been coming to Anticipation.

'Where's Mario?' she demanded, as soon as she got the chance.

'He got an unexpected offer to go to Queensland, and your Mario—he loves the sun,' said the tall guy with a grin. 'Don't worry, though. He told me exactly what kind of music to play, if I didn't want you lot to slaughter me. I'm Larry, by the way.'

Carole ducked her head and turned away. He needn't think he could win her over that easily. She was sure her evening was ruined, because she didn't feel in the mood for any more changes.

But just then Gee and the rest of the group surged in, grinning and waving. Carole's spirits soared again and she reached for Drew's hand. Maybe she'd have a good time after all.

Chapter 5

Carole woke late on Saturday morning. She wandered out into the lounge room, still humming the last song of the night, and found Mish curled up on the cushions in a nest made from the Saturday paper.

She dropped the section she was holding and glanced up at Carole with a strange look. 'Your father called,' she said awkwardly. 'He wanted to know whether you'd have lunch with him today, because he's leaving for America tomorrow.'

'Oh yeah? He's left it a bit late, hasn't he? Suppose I was already having lunch with someone else.'

'Are you?' asked Mish with the glimmer of a smile.

'No ... but I might be.'

'Well, ring your father when you've made up your mind,' Mish said firmly and returned to the paper.

Carole stomped angrily around the flat, collecting her breakfast and then trying to decide on a place to settle. At moments like these she missed her old home more than ever. If she'd felt mad or miserable, she could've hidden herself in the sunroom or the breakfast nook or out on the patio, until her bad mood passed. But in this tiny flat there was virtually no privacy. She was under Mish's eye, unless she went off to her bedroom, and there was something a bit too childish about that.

In the end she went outside, balancing her cereal bowl on the balcony railing and staring out at the city skyline, until the woman next door came out to water her pot plants. Muttering under her breath, Carole stormed inside again and dialled her dad's number with sharp stabs of her finger.

At the sound of his voice, however, her rage melted away on the spot. 'Yes, lunch'd be great,' she told him happily. 'No, of course I want to see you. That restaurant near the park sounds terrific. Right, I'll meet you outside the flats in an hour's time.'

When she put down the phone, Mish's golden head was bent over the paper, as if to show that she hadn't been listening in. Carole felt a surge of sympathy for her. The tiny flat must be difficult for Mish, too.

'What are you going to do today?' she asked.

'Oh, I don't know,' Mish said vaguely. 'I might write a few letters or go down to one of the markets to see if there's any cheap cane

41

furniture.'

'Leave it till tomorrow and I'll come with you,' Carole suggested.

Mish brightened. 'That'd be fun. Just like old times—remember how we chose the furniture for your room together?' They both remembered Carole's room and Mish's face fell again. 'You don't have to come, though, Carole. I mean, if you want to go to Gee's or something ... '

'Hang about,' Carole interrupted. 'Since when did you start wondering whether you were good company? We'll have a great time. I can see Gee any day of the week—I'd much rather go looking round markets with you.'

Now I've cheered up one of my parents, she thought as she went to get changed. Let's see what sort of state the other one's in.

Her dad seemed to be in a pretty good mood as they drove down to the restaurant. 'That's a nice dress,' he told her appreciatively. 'You'll turn all the businessmen's heads.'

Carole felt a momentary twinge. She'd already realised it was lucky she'd always spent so much money on clothes, since she probably wouldn't be buying many more for a while.

But, she told herself firmly, she needn't think about money today. She'd always paid her way with boyfriends, and she didn't intend to change that, no matter how poor she was now. It was all right to let her dad buy her a meal though—in fact, she had every intention of ordering the most expensive dish on the menu.

Still, it seemed a bit weird to order lobster when her dad knew that she preferred roast chicken, and in the end she decided not to make a fuss. Beside, she was feeling too comfortable, with the waiters coming over regularly to check on their needs and the lake sparkling brightly outside the plate glass windows.

'Well,' her dad said heartily, 'how are things?' Carole was just about to tell him when he added in a rush, 'Everything going well at school? Do you think you're properly prepared for the exams?'

'Oh, you know me. I never like to leave things till the last minute.'

'That's my girl. I'm glad everything's working out for you. What do you want me to bring you back from America? It'll be a post-exam present, so you can ask for anything you want.'

Carole looked at him, startled. 'But it's still ages before the exams. How long are you going for?'

'It's an important trip, you know. I'm supposed to go around to a range of firms like ours, in a number of different states, and that sort of thing can't be done in a rush. It's not just a question of studying their business methods. I'll also be trying to build links between us, which means that I'll be meeting their top men—and women too, of course—and spending time with them socially.'

His voice trailed away as Carole continued to stare at him blankly. 'So how long will you be away?' she repeated.

'Over six weeks.' He shifted his cutlery around a bit and then said, 'But you can ring me if you need to talk about anything. The firm will always know where I am.'

Carole felt her eyes growing moist and she blinked quickly. 'Thanks a lot,' she said sarcastically. 'I'm sure that'll be a great help.'

Somehow the conversation never recovered after that. They both did their best—Carole forced herself to ask some more questions about the trip and her dad enquired about Gee, who was a great favourite of his, and Drew, who wasn't.

But every other avenue seemed to lead back to the forbidden topic of her parents' separation. Carole had dreaded having to talk about it, except that not talking about it was even worse. By the time the car stopped outside the flats again, she was so steamed up that she burst out, 'Are you seeing anyone else, Dad?'

Her dad jerked back as if she'd slapped him. 'No, I am not. Whatever gave you that idea? If either of us was likely to do that sort of thing it'd be your mother, not me.'

'Mish isn't seeing anybody,' Carole said indignantly. 'I can tell you, I'd know if she was.'

Her dad's shoulders relaxed and she realised with annoyance that he'd been fishing for the information. Oh well, she didn't care. At least she'd found out what she wanted to know. She was glad that there was no one else involved, even though it made the whole thing more puzzling.

'Anyhow, I don't know why you were surprised at me for asking,' she said sulkily. 'That's the reason most people's parents break up, after all.'

Her dad gave her one of his steely looks. 'Well, I'm not "most parents",' he said crushingly. 'We'll talk about all of this when I get back from America, Carole. And in the meantime—well, Mish insists that she won't take any money from me, so I won't force it on her, but I wanted you to have this, for your Christmas presents and so on.'

He pressed a folded note into Carole's hand. Her first feeling was one of relief but it was closely followed by a feeling of alarm.

'No, no, I'll be back in Australia for Christmas, of course,' her dad said, reading the expression on her face. 'You could always have Christmas dinner with me, if you'd like to.'

'Thanks,' Carole mumbled. She kissed her dad quickly and leapt out of the car, bolting up the steps without looking back.

More than ever, she wanted somewhere private to go to. Finally she locked herself in the laundry and burst into tears. There she went, feeling torn between her parents again. How could she leave Mish on Christmas Day, when all of Mish's family lived interstate? But her father had no family at all—except that all his business friends would probably still invite him to share their Christmas. Then again, Mish might've made a whole heap of new friends by then ...

It was all too much. Carole couldn't see how she was going to decide. She could only see that Christmas was likely to be the unhappiest time of the year, instead of the happiest. She let the person outside rattle the laundry door three times before she finally wiped her eyes and let herself out.

'Sorry,' she mumbled, head bent, before she bolted up the stairs.

When she opened the flat door, Mish jumped and pushed the typewriter away, dropping the cover over the half-finished page. 'Have a nice lunch?' she asked brightly.

'Not really.' Carole scowled. 'Dad's impossible. I don't know how you managed to put up with him for so long. He wouldn't talk about anything and—and he would've been away for the whole of my exams. Some father!'

Mish gave her a troubled look. 'Carole, don't get the idea that you'll be pleasing me if you start hating Roger. I certainly don't hate him, you know. Okay, he can drive me mad, but I drive him mad too, remember. It's not a case of either of us being right or wrong. We're both doing what's right for us. It's just that the two things are incompatible.'

'I don't hate him on your behalf,' Carole grumbled. 'I'm perfectly capable of hating him for my own sake.'

But she smiled as she said it, and Mish looked

relieved. 'I know he can be irritating,' she said with a grin. 'But hate—what's he done to deserve that?'

'Well, for one thing he's sitting pretty—taking me to posh restaurants and going home to a nice house—while we're stuck in this hole.'

'He earned his nice house,' Mish reminded her. 'And I don't feel as though I've got any claim to it. After all, he supported me for years and I just took it for granted. It's taken me until now to realise that he had a right to ask something from me in return.'

'Like what?' Carole asked, puzzled.

'You must've picked up on some of what we were fighting about,' Mish said wryly. 'Roger wanted me to entertain his business contacts, and I kept telling him I was no good at that sort of thing. I'm not the hostess type—I wanted to go on fixing the house and restoring furniture, just like I'd done when we were younger and had less money. That was all right while Roger and I were getting on well, I suppose, but once we began to fight, I felt as though I was just freeloading off him.'

Carole frowned. Something about this didn't sound right to her, but she couldn't put it into words. 'At least you could've taken a bit of money from him, just to get yourself started,' she suggested doubtfully.

'Oh well, there'll be a divorce settlement some day,' Mish said vaguely. 'The lawyers can decide all that. As for now, I've got enough money of my own to see us through, even though there's not a lot to spare for luxuries.' She hesitated and added, 'There's only one thing I'm sorry about. It's not going to be much of a Christmas for you this year, Carole.'

'Oh, that's fine,' Carole said firmly.

On the spot she decided that, one way or another, she was going to get some money together and make this Christmas the most fantastic they'd ever had.

Chapter 6

Carole waited until she was in her bedroom to unfold the note her dad had given her. She looked down at it and whistled softly. A hundred dollar note—she couldn't remember seeing one of those before. That should solve all her problems.

But even before she'd started to draw up her list of expenses, she found herself remembering how much she'd spent with Drew the night before. The wonderful note would only cover five evenings with Drew—or less, if he was in an extravagant mood.

For a moment Carole slipped back into wondering whether she really needed to insist on paying her own way. Principles aside, though, there was no point in wondering. She'd had to argue with Drew for a while to get him to see things her way, but these days he never wasted his time offering. If she wanted to change his mind again, she'd have to tell him outright to pay for her—and she couldn't do that.

'There's a simple solution, though,' she said out loud. 'He could just agree to spend less money when we go out together.'

Without noticing, she'd started to bite her fingernails again, a habit she had broken years ago. Hastily she pulled her hand away from her mouth and sat on it. (She'd never heard of anyone else curing themselves of nail-biting this way, but it always worked for her.) Then she sighed, realising she must be really worried. And she knew perfectly well what she was worried about.

Drew wasn't likely to agree easily to the idea that they should cut down on the amount they spent. And after all, why should he? His motto was, 'If you've got it, spend it,' and he'd still got it. Only Carole was in trouble.

Come to think of it, she'd never thought about the whole question of money until it *was* her trouble. Looking back, she wondered guiltily whether she'd pushed other people into paying more than they could afford. How many kids had dropped out of their group because they couldn't hack the pace? How many kids had she never got to know because they could see that her idea of a fun time was to spend money like water?

Gritting her teeth, Carole drew up two budgets. One listed the things she would need for her dream Christmas—the cost of a tree with beautiful decorations, an enormous turkey, a Christmas cake, a pudding and presents for Mish and all her friends. Of course she didn't know the price of everything, but she had a sinking feeling that this list alone would use up the note her dad had given her twice over.

Then there was the Drew budget. That was simpler—she just estimated the amount of money she usually spent with him, counted the weeks to Christmas and multiplied one number by the others. As she jotted down the answer, she could feel her heart sinking. The hundred dollar note which had seemed to promise so much now looked like spare change.

'I can't believe I used to spend so much money without thinking about it,' she moaned.

No doubt about it, she'd have to get some more money from somewhere. It was awful to be poor while she was still surrounded by all her expensive dresses and jewellery.

Dresses and jewellery! Carole jumped to her feet and ran to the cupboard. There was the dress she'd worn to the Leland Ladies College dance—and the dress she'd worn to have lunch at her dad's club—and a dozen other dresses which cost a mint and which she wasn't likely to wear again, not in her new life. Then there were some of the weirder items she'd bought with Drew, clothes which were so unusual and striking that you couldn't wear them every week. A lot of those could go, too.

In the end she had a big pile of expensive clothes, all in great condition. She stepped back, hands on hips, and looked down at them. There was a shop in the city called Good As New which sold classy second-hand clothes—she and Gee had browsed around it once, and Gee even bought a shirt for a giggle, though her mum wouldn't let her wear it. The Good As New prices were pretty high, so Carole thought she ought to get a reasonable sum for her stuff. It might even solve all her money problems.

She was about to tidy the clothes away when there was a tap on her door and Mish came in. Carole jumped guiltily, but luckily Mish didn't seem to notice.

'Oh, you bought all those lovely clothes with you,' she said, looking concerned. 'Honestly, darling, I don't know that you'll be getting much chance to wear them—except when you go out with Drew, of course.'

'Well, they're not much use to Dad,' Carole pointed out, pleased with herself for thinking of a snappy answer. 'Actually, I was just about to pack them away in the top of the cupboard, except I thought I'd iron them first.'

She felt even more pleased with herself. Now she could iron the clothes openly, without Mish asking difficult questions. And she'd stopped Mish from wondering where the clothes had disappeared to.

Not that Mish was paying much attention. 'That's nice,' she said vaguely. 'Now listen, I've kept forgetting to give you pocket money, and I realised that you've been too thoughtful to ask. So ...'

'It's all right,' Carole said awkwardly. 'Dad gave me some money today.'

'Oh, but you should keep that to buy yourself a treat, something to make you feel better,' Mish insisted. 'I'll take care of your day to day expenses. We're not flat broke yet, I promise.'

'But we will be soon,' Carole guessed. Her recent experience had helped her understand Mish's position better, and she added warmly, 'Mish, if you start to get worried about the money situation, you'll tell me, won't you?'

Mish waved her hand airily. 'I've got a few ideas in mind, Carole. I don't intend to start worrying just yet.'

Carole looked at her mum with protective affection. In the big shirt she'd worn to paint their bookshelves in bright pastel colours, Mish seemed more like her older sister than ever. It was possible that Mish wouldn't feel they needed to worry until they were actually living under a bridge.

And it was extremely possible that Mish would think it was a great joke if their Christmas dinner consisted of a tin of tuna and some frozen peas. Carole couldn't do much about keeping a roof over their heads, but at least she could make sure their Christmas was better than that.

She couldn't bear to wait until the next weekend before taking her clothes in to Good As New. So on Tuesday she carried them to school and hid them in her locker. (Now she was going to school by train, it was easier to manage this without Gee noticing.)

Then in the afternoon, just before singing practice started, she faked an attack of cramps, but instead of going to the sick-room she collected her gear and headed straight for the gate, heart pounding. It was the first time Carole had ever skipped a lesson, but she told herself with a wry smile that it made up for all the singing practices she'd pretended to be attending last week.

She found the shop easily and walked in, trying to look confident. At the last minute it occurred to her that she might've been better off to change out of her uniform, but it was too late to do anything about that. She'd look even weirder if she walked in wearing a long dance dress, after all.

She had to wait for five minutes while the woman behind the counter jotted down figures in a book. Carole's palms were beginning to sweat by the time she looked up and said, 'Now, how can I help you?'

'I've brought some clothes to sell.' Her voice had come out in a squeak, so she swallowed and tried again. 'I wondered if you could tell me how much money you'd give me for them.'

Her voice was a low growl this time, but at least the woman hadn't fallen on the floor in fits of laughter. However, she was tossing the clothes around as if she was examining a collection of old dish rags.

'I'm afraid we don't hand over the money

when you bring in the clothes,' she said finally.

Carole stared at her in disbelief. 'Why not?'

'Well, if we were an ordinary dress shop, we'd return any clothes we didn't sell to the manufacturers. In our case, if the clothes don't sell, we return them to you. This is a business, you know. We aren't running a charity.'

'Oh, right. I see.' Carole hesitated. 'Well, how much would I get, supposing I sold all of these?'

The woman tumbled through the clothes again and named an amount that made Carole's eyes fly open.

'But they cost hundreds of dollars altogether, when they were new,' she protested. 'Most of them have only been worn a few times. How come you can't pay me more than that?'

'They're not new now,' the woman pointed out. 'People simply won't pay high prices for second-hand clothes, however good. Fashions change, as I'm sure you've noticed. And of course we take fifty percent of the price as well. But we do good business here—you won't get a better offer anywhere else.'

Carole stared at her silently and after a few seconds the woman asked her snappily to make up her mind. With a sigh she nodded agreement. It would've been a different matter if she'd been really fond of any of the clothes, but Mish was right—she certainly didn't need them now. Better to earn a little money than none at all.

All the same, a little money wasn't going to make much difference to her overall problems.

She was still faced with the same need to finance her dream Christmas, not to mention her relationship with Drew. Carole had the feeling that she needn't waste her time trying to sell her jewellery. Second-hand chains and bracelets probably went by the same rules as second-hand clothes, and her jewellery would be a real sacrifice, since every piece she owned was a present from Dad or Mish or Drew.

No, there was only one thing to be done. She'd have to get a job. On her way home in the bus, Carole schemed away. She was sure she'd be good at all sorts of things. She could work in a shop or a MacDonalds or a factory—she'd be glad to do anything for pay.

Then, as she walked up the street towards the block of flats, reality hit her like a bucket of cold water. She couldn't take a job while she was studying for the exams. Mish would hardly be rapt to know that her daughter had given her a wonderful Christmas by throwing away all her years of schooling.

And come to think of it, she couldn't even get a weekend job without Mish knowing, and part of her plan was to give Mish a terrific surprise. Of course, she could think up some other reason for finding a holiday job—saving for next year or something—but there wasn't a lot of time left after the exams, and Carole doubted whether she could save quickly enough.

A Christmas dinner bank loan? Write to her relatives in Sydney? Tell Drew it was all over and do the best she could with the hundred dollars? Buy a turkey chick and raise it secretly in the laundry?

Carole could feel her brain running wild. As she ran up the stairs, she told herself to forget the whole thing and come back to it when her thoughts were clearer.

But somehow over the rest of the week her thoughts never seemed to get any clearer. On one level she went on behaving as normal—listening carefully in class, preparing steadily for the exams, chatting with Gee or Mish. Underneath all of this, though, she felt like there was a great yawning blank, waiting to swallow her up.

By Friday Carole was so depressed that, when Gee brought up the subject of the girls' night out at Anticipation, she just said flatly, 'I can't go. I haven't got enough money.'

'Oh-oh!' said Gee. 'So there's something else you haven't been telling me. I was starting to wonder about that. We'll have a talk about this later on, but don't worry about Anticipation. I can fix that.'

'How?' Carole asked, but Gee only looked mysterious. 'You're not going to pay for me yourself, are you? Because if so, then you're a real mate and everything, but it wouldn't really solve the problem and I couldn't accept it.'

'No, my idea is much better than that,' Gee answered, and that was all she'd tell her. In the end Carole was so curious that she decided that it was worth a trip into the city, if only to see what

Gee would do.

In actual fact, she *didn't* get to see what Gee would do. They arrived early at Anticipation and Gee told her to wait in the foyer. Five minutes later she came out of the office with the manager and Larry, the new DJ, the three of them full of smiles.

'Carole Carmody,' the manager announced, 'in recognition of all the years you've been coming to this disco, I award you a lifetime's free pass. Larry, will you make the presentation?'

The lanky DJ handed her a printed card with a flourish and unexpectedly bent to kiss her on the cheek. 'From all I've heard, you really deserve this,' he said. 'Enjoy—and keep up the great dancing, Caro.'

Carole was blushing wildly. She clutched the pass and stammered out her thanks, which made the two guys look almost as embarrassed as she did. They faded hastily away, leaving Carole with Gee.

'What did you say to them?' Carole wailed.

'Don't get in a state. I didn't tell them your life story or anything. I'm not totally tasteless. I just mentioned that you mightn't be able to come to the disco any more, for financial reasons, and they managed to work the rest out for themselves. Mind you, they did exactly what I would've done in their place,' Gee added smugly.

'Gee, you're amazing.' Carole sighed.

It gave her a warm feeling inside to think of how her friend had responded to her troubles.

You couldn't feel totally down with someone like Gee around. Despite everything, Carole knew she was was going to have a great evening. And something was giving things an extra sparkle, except that it took her a moment to work out what it was.

Oh, that's right. Larry had called her Caro. She had a nickname at last.

Chapter 7

Just as she'd guessed, Carole had a terrific time. After all her worries about Drew, it was kind of restful to dance with a whole range of guys, returning to Gee and her friends in between times.

The group took it for granted that the main aim of the evening was for them to have fun together. So Carole was a bit surprised when she noticed that a good-looking guy was keeping a close watch on Gee. Then she realised that Gee was secretly trying to shoo him away, and she grinned at her friend.

'Looks like Sean's so crazy about you that he can't even stay away for the girls' night out,' she whispered.

'Sean? Oh I broke up with Sean last week. He's going out with Anne now. That's Mike over there. I met him in the supermarket last weekend and he seemed really nice, but now I'm not so sure he's my type. You know, Lucy's always complaining that she never meets guys who want to get really serious. I wonder ...'

Gee looked thoughtfully from Lucy to Mike and Carole giggled to herself. She was going to stick around and see what happened next, but just then Larry put on one of her favourite songs. She caught the eye of a guy standing nearby, and a second later she was out on the floor, lost in the music.

Larry was a great DJ. Carole wondered how she could ever have doubted it. He'd taken careful note of Mario's suggestions, so there wasn't a sudden change in the music at Anticipation. But he introduced some of his own tastes as well, and Carole found herself appreciating it more and more. Plus which, he had a lively way of talking which seemed to draw everyone together and give the night extra excitement.

Carole felt really high. When she noticed Lucy and Mike dancing close together, she laughed so hard it was difficult to stop. Her partner looked at her questioningly, but she couldn't explain to him why she found it so funny, so in the end she excused herself and went to look for Gee.

She came across her friend, dancing equally close with a blond spunk. Carole chuckled softly. Gee had obviously fallen in love again already. Carole was in too good a mood to want to interrupt her. Instead she leaned against the wall to watch the swirling lights, the fast-moving dancers ... and Larry.

But Gee appeared beside her soon after. 'It's getting late,' she said regretfully. 'If you want to have that talk, we'd better head off to the coffee shop next door.'

'No worries. You can always ring me tomorrow or something.'

Gee looked indignant. 'You think I'm the kind of person who'd dump her best friend for some guy she'd just met? No way, Carole. You wanted to talk to me, so that's what's going to happen. Either this guy'll be happy to see me when I'm ready to see him, or else I'm not interested in him anyway.'

Carole gazed at her friend admiringly. She had a feeling that, if Gee was in her position, she'd manage to turn those problems with Drew into something really simple.

'You've got it all sorted out haven't you?' she asked with a sigh.

'I keep telling you, if there was a school subject called Guys, I'd get good marks for once,' Gee said with a twinkle. 'Mind you, I wouldn't say I had it all sorted out. There's more to life than guys—like history, languages and English, to start with.'

'Oh, school! That's easy.'

'For you, maybe. We all feel confident about different things. If it makes you feel any better, I'm not sure what I'd do if I met a guy who really appealed to me more than the others.'

Carole tried to imagine Gee being as anxious for some guy's approval as the rest of her friends often were. She was starting to smile when Gee added, 'Of course, after all the guys I've been out with, I'd only think a guy was special if he was totally right for me. And in that case, there's an even chance that I was totally right for him, too.'

Carole burst out laughing. 'I reckon that's true. Oh well, I'll have to stop hoping you'll meet your match one day—unless it's your perfect match. I'd better just concentrate on the things I'm confident about ... whatever they are.'

'For starters, we'd better build up your confidence about this money stuff. Come on, I always think more creatively over a good capuccino.'

As Gee drew patterns on the foam of her coffee, Carole explained to her how she'd decided that she wanted to give Mish a Christmas to remember.

'But that sort of thing takes money,' she ended, 'and money's in pretty short supply since Dad and Mish separated.'

'You mean your dad went off and left you flat broke?' said Gee her dark eyes flashing.

'Oh, no,' Carole said quickly. 'He gave me some money but I need that for other things. I don't want to impose on Mish, you see—she says she's got some savings but I don't know how long they'll last.'

She fidgeted uncomfortably with her coffee spoon, aware that she was deliberately giving Gee the wrong impression. From the way she was telling it, Gee would assume she was nobly refusing Mish's money—and she wasn't.

On the other hand, she'd had to admit that her dad hadn't forgotten her, because otherwise Gee would've thought badly of him, which wouldn't have been fair. But if she said directly that both her parents had tried to make sure she was taken care of, then Gee would've been bound to ask questions—and Carole wasn't prepared to let Gee know that half her budget was set aside for her times with Drew.

She wasn't sure why she was being so secretive. Gee would probably have some great suggestion that'd solve her problems with Drew. Except that Gee might suggest she told Drew that if he wasn't prepared to cut down on his extravagant ways, then she wasn't interested. That might work for Gee, but Carole already knew that it wouldn't work for her. She didn't have boyfriends queuing up for her, the way Gee did.

She returned from her thoughts to find Gee watching her patiently. 'I said, how come this whole business about Christmas is so important to you?' Gee repeated.

Carole stared back. 'What do you mean? Christmas just *is* important. Or isn't it the same in Italian families?'

'That shows how much you know about Italian families.' Gee chuckled. 'My uncle even comes to church with us at Christmas and that doesn't happen every day of the year. And we have our traditional food and things, just like you do ... But all the same, with Nonna's last illness, nobody really noticed that it happened on Christmas Day. We just dropped all that stuff and gathered around her, because that was more important.'

Carole frowned. She suspected Gee was sending her some kind of message, except that she wasn't sure what it meant.

'Well even if I can't explain it properly, I'd still like to have a wonderful Christmas this year,' she said stubbornly.

She expected Gee to go on arguing, but Gee just smiled at her. 'Fair enough. Then we'll just have to think of ways for you to earn money.'

Carole told Gee about all the plans she'd tried or discarded so far. She'd been around the shops and priced everything, so she was able to tell Gee how much she needed, as well.

'Basically, I've got enough money to buy the turkey so far, but it'll look pretty lonely by itself,' she finished gloomily.

Gee thought for a moment. 'I can see that getting a job isn't really the go,' she said. 'Have you got anything else you could sell? When my oldest brother was getting married, he took a small stall at one of those trash and treasure markets and flogged his guitar and heaps of other stuff he didn't want any more. He didn't have to give half his profits to the shopowner, like you did with Good As New, so he did pretty well out of it.'

'Well, I suppose I could've done that if I'd still been living at home,' Carole said doubtfully. 'But the flat's so tiny that basically I only brought my clothes and books. I was lucky that I even had some clothes to sell. Maybe I should get them back from Good As New and try a trash and treasure stall instead?'

'No, you probably need a bigger range of things to make it worthwhile. Still, the idea reminds me of something.' Gee clicked her fingers impatiently for a moment and then exclaimed, 'Markets! Why don't we think of something you can make and sell at a market?'

'Hey, that's fantastic. But what could I do?'

'You could knit jumpers.'

'In summer? Besides, I'm the slowest knitter on earth.'

'Well then, you could paint T-shirts.'

'Oh yeah? Remember me in art classes?'

Gee giggled. 'I remember. Okay, you could make pottery mugs. You were good at that.'

'One small problem. I don't have a kiln tucked away in my bedroom.'

'All right, then,' Gee said, annoyed. 'If you don't like any of my suggestions, what can you do?'

'Well it's not like I can't do anything,' Carole snapped back. 'I *can* make ace earrings. You know that perfectly well, 'cause I made the pair you're wearing.'

'There you are,' Gee said grinning. 'Earrings are a fantastic idea. You can make them in your spare time, and it'll be easy to keep it secret from Mish, because if she comes into your room unexpectedly, you can just say they're Christmas presents for your friends. Come to think of it, that could solve the problem of your Christmas presents, too!'

'And I could make special Christmas earrings,' Carole added, warming to the idea. 'I could use big red and green sequins—or I could get sheets of thin plastic and cut out holly leaf shapes, or — '

'Hold it,' Gee cut in. 'Why don't we hit the shops tomorrow and spend the afternoon trying different ideas? Then you can order what you need in bulk and build up a good collection in time for the Christmas shoppers.'

'Sounds fine to me,' Carole said happily. 'Thanks, Gee. You're a real friend.'

Chapter 8

Despite all the dancing the night before, Carole woke early the next morning. She tried to eat her breakfast as slowly as possible but it was gone in a flash. She fidgeted about for a while longer and then snatched up the phone to call Gee.

'Who's that?' Gee said sleepily, when she finally came to the phone.

'It's me,' Carole told her. 'I just wanted to know whether the plans for today were still on.'

Carole could almost hear the wheels of Gee's brain turning slowly before she said, 'Today. Oh right, today. Yeah, it's still on—but in my opinion, today hasn't even started yet!'

'That's what you think. We've got heaps of places to visit, so we better get a move on. I'll be round in three quarters of an hour.'

Humming cheerfully, Carole made another cup of coffee and carried it in to her mum. 'I'm going out with Gee,' she said. 'I'll be home about mid-afternoon, and then I'm going out with Drew.'

'That's nice.' Mish yawned. 'Where are you and Gee off to?'

'Oh just out.'

Mish chuckled. 'Now I know why I used to drive my mum mad. All right, keep your secrets. I'm not the least bit curious. I'll just trail you everywhere you go in the ute, that's all.'

'No, you won't,' Carole said with a grin. 'You'll roll over and go to sleep again, knowing you.'

'Not necessarily.' Mish tried to look as dignified as she could in an old T-shirt, with her gold hair standing on end. 'I've got things to do as well, missy.'

'Oh yeah? Where are you going?'

'Out,' Mish said smugly, and they both laughed.

Carole always enjoyed prowling around shops that sold beads and trimmings, and Gee could turn any kind of shopping trip into an adventure. They travelled across three suburbs, pricing different beads and sequins and raving away as they went. By the time they reached the final shop on Carole's list, a place that sold a truly incredible range of beads, the young guy behind the counter told them apologetically that he was closing up in five minutes.

Carole started to hurry around the shelves. Behind her, she could hear Gee explaining their story to the guy, and after a while they both joined her. He seemed suddenly eager to display every red and green sparkle in the shop, although he kept giving the samples to Gee instead of to Carole.

When Carole picked up her parcels and headed for the door, she found her friend had stayed behind for a last conversation.

'Well, we both did pretty well out of that shopping spree,' she said with a grin as Gee joined her outside. 'I thought you were seeing that blond guy, though.'

Gee shook her dark curls vigorously. 'He got the sulks when I said I was having coffee with you, and I told you how I feel about that sort of thing. Colin's different. He reckoned it was great that I was spending the morning helping you with your business.'

'Of course he did,' Carole teased. 'He never would've met you otherwise.'

'Oh, we would've met somehow,' Gee said earnestly. 'If you're meant to meet someone, then it happens, I really believe that.'

If anyone else had said this, Carole would've just laughed. But with Gee she knew it was possible. Not that she could see Colin as the sort of person Gee would be drawn to by some mysterious force. He'd been really helpful and everything, but he wasn't Gee's usual hunky type.

But she soon forgot all about Colin as she started to make plans about the earrings. The moment they got to the Corelli's house, she spilled out the glittering contents of the various bags across the lounge room table and started to match up beads and sequins.

Gee had decided to give her hair a henna treatment, so she wandered in and out with her head swathed in Glad Wrap, giving Carole her opinions. Silvana had her say as well, and even Gee's brother Paul came and looked over her shoulder.

'That's n-nice,' he said with an effort, pointing at the holly leaf Carole had just cut from a sheet of green plastic. 'If you w-warm it in the oven, you could b-bend it a bit, give it a better ...'

He struggled with the final word and as usual Carole found herself hurrying in to help him. 'A better shape. That's true, Paul. Let's give it a go.'

They practised for a while and, after one accident with Mrs Corelli's oven trays, they produced a reasonable holly leaf.

'You know, I think that's the best of the lot,' Carole said, pleased. 'With these little beads for holly berries, it'll look stunninng.'

'Can you m-make one to sh-sh-?'

'To show you? No problem.'

Paul watched with close attention as Carole's fingers worked away nimbly. He was in second year at university, doing as brilliantly in maths as he had at school, plus, he was a star soccer player with shoulders to match. He was just the sort of guy Carole usually felt intimidated by—but how could you feel intimidated by a guy whose sentences you finished for him?

'That's great,' he said now. 'Can I have a t-try?'

Silvana and Gee drifted back in again and soon

71

they were all sitting around, heads bent over the beads as they fitted them onto the earring hooks. The Corelli sisters tried on the finished earrings immediately and paraded round the room, turning their heads this way and that.

'Terrific,' Silvana approved. 'Let me have a dozen and I'll flog them to all my friends. They love this kind of fun stuff.'

Carole beamed. 'Thanks, Sil. And for starters, I want to give those two pairs to you and Gee, for all the work you've done today. Paul, would you like a pair to give to your girlfriend?'

'Haven't got a g-g-g ...'

'Well you might, by Christmas time,' Carole said with a grin, but Paul shook his head, so she packed them away. When she looked up, Silvana and Gee were standing with their purses ready.

'We're not taking presents from you,' Gee told her. 'If you're going into business, then you have to start right now, okay?'

Carole argued back but the Corellis insisted. 'You can't hand out earrings to all your friends and still make a profit,' Silvana told her firmly, and Carole had to admit she could see her point.

'Then I'll just have to thank you even more,' she said.

'No need,' Gee told her. 'It's been fun.'

'You could w-work around here every weekend, if you don't want your m-mum to know what you're doing,' Paul offered. 'We'd be happy to h-h-'

'To help me? Oh no, I couldn't land myself on

you like that,' Carole protested. 'I'm the one who wants to raise the money, so I'm the one who has to do the work from now on.'

She was still feeling pleased with herself when Drew came to collect her that night, and she found herself pouring out the whole story. Drew looked at her, puzzled.

'Making earrings like holly leaves? Selling them at the market? Why would you want to do that, Carole?'

Too late, she realised where the conversation might lead her. 'Oh I thought it might be fun,' she said lamely. Drew eyed her strangely but to her relief he didn't say any more about it, and as they set off to the movies he started to talk about his week at school.

Carole had suggested that they go and see a film in the hopes that this would make the evening less expensive than usual. It was a good idea, except that after the movie Drew wanted to catch the supper show at a comedy theatre in the city, and then it was so late that he suggested a taxi home.

Carole fully intended to smile and say 'Yes.' After all, she'd decided she wasn't going to discuss money with Drew, and she intended to stick to it. But she was tired, and her purse was emptying at an alarming rate, and although she tried to speak her bottom lip was trembling so much she was afraid she might burst into tears instead.

Drew must have sensed something, because

he said unexpectedly, 'I'll pay for it, of course.'

Carole felt an instant surge of hope, but then her pride took over. She realised that at another time she might've accepted the offer, since it was Drew's idea, after all. But, now she really needed the money, so of course she squared her shoulders and said, 'No, that's fine. I'll go halves.'

As soon as she got home, she sat down at her desk and drew up her budget again. It looked even worse than before. She was feeling tired already from her long morning shopping and her long evening with Drew, but wearily she picked up the template Paul had made for her and began to cut holly shapes from a sheet of green plastic.

Chapter 9

Carole had sometimes felt embarrassed about studying so hard. It wasn't that she tried to suck up to the teachers. If anything, she really admired the people who wrote up their projects the night before they were due, or crammed for exams in the final week.

'Remember, though, you can't believe everything you hear,' Mish warned her when she was talking about this one day. 'I used to talk big when I was at school. I never let on I was doing any work—but even if I dashed off my essays at the last minute, I'd always done heaps of reading and thinking beforehand.'

That made Carole feel a bit better, but at any rate there was nothing she could do about it. Her brain simply wasn't built for speed. If she worked consistently all year, she was fine. If she tried to run too close to the deadline, she went into a spin and lost it.

So in the weeks before her final exams, she only had to read through her detailed notes and fix them in her mind. At least she could be confident she'd done the best she was capable of, and after that it was up to the examiners to decide what they thought. It was lucky she had one area of confidence, Carole thought gloomily, because the rest of her life was a mess.

Making earrings wasn't quite as simple as it sounded. To begin with, she'd had to work out in detail how many earrings she'd have to make to earn the money she needed, how much she should charge for them and how much the materials would cost. The maths of it all was no problem to Carole, but she kept forgetting to include expenses like the hire of the stall at the market, so she had to do the whole sum three or four times.

Then she had to buy plastic and beads and hooks in bulk, which made a big hole in the hundred dollars and left her feeling really worried. Okay, the money would come back to her in the end, but in the meantime she had very little cash left at all.

Luckily, Drew was the kind of student who left everything till the last minute. So over the next few weeks he and Carole mostly met up on Saturday afternoons, to walk by the river or have coffee in one of the local cafes before Drew went back to slave away at his books. This was a relief for Carole, because it basically left her savings intact, but she could see she was putting off the showdown. After the exams, she was going to be in real trouble.

And even before the exams, she didn't feel too great. Her revision programme was under control, but it still took time, and so did the earrings. Her fingers were covered with cuts from the Stanley knife, where her hand had slipped from sheer exhaustion. Her fingertips were bruised from pushing the hooks through the plastic. Her whole body ached from lack of sleep.

Still, there were a few bright moments in among the grey ones. Most of them at Anticipation. For one thing, it was somewhere she could have fun without worrying about money. Carole's free pass was like a lifeline to her in those days. It was a sign that people cared about her, even people who didn't know her as well as Gee did.

Of course, even the free pass got her into a bit of trouble. When Drew first saw her using it, he stared and asked accusingly where it came from. Carole froze. For once she couldn't think up a good story on the spur of the moment.

Luckily, Gee was standing right behind them in the queue. She leaned over Drew's shoulder and said, 'Oh, weren't you there the night they were giving out free passes? Carole answered the hardest question of the night, so she got a lifetime's pass.'

'It's not fair,' Drew grumbled. 'I've been coming to Anticipation for ages, and I have to miss out on the one night when they give away something really good. What was the question, Carole?'

Carole's brain was back in working order again. Remembering that Larry liked the music of the fifties, she thought of one of her dad's favourite singers. 'I had to say who sang "Town Without Pity," she told Drew. 'The answer's Gene Pitney.'

Drew shrugged. 'Never heard of her.'

'Him,' said Carole smugly. 'It's G-e-n-e, not J-e-a-n.'

'Never heard of him, either,' Drew said with a grin. 'Looks like you can keep your lifetime's pass, after all.'

'Thanks—for nothing,' Carole said, relaxing again, and soon they were out on the dance floor and she could forget about her worries for another few hours.

But inevitably the worries crept back again when she arrived home. All her drawers were full of holly earrings, carefully wrapped in layers of tissue paper, and yet she was still falling behind on her quota. As she got more tired, she got clumsier. Her fingers wouldn't fit the hooks into the leaves, she dropped the shiny red beads when she was trying to stick them on and all in all she was starting to feel totally incompetent.

The week before her exams, Carole hardly had the strength to keep going. At the same time her plans had a grip on her. Having drawn up her time line, she was too tired to think of how she could change it. She could only keep on plodding on, doing everything slowly and badly, but feeling that at least she was doing something.

Carole was counting on Saturday evening to give her a chance to catch up and get some rest. Then Drew rang towards the end of the week, suggesting that they go to Anticipation.

'No!' Carole said in a panic. 'No, I don't want to.'

'Ah, come on, it's just what you need. It'll give you a bit of a lift, so you can breeze through the exams. Don't tell me you need time to prepare, I know you better than that. You probably could've sat for the exams last month without any problems.'

These days I can't do a thing without any problems, Carole thought sadly. Aloud, she said, 'Listen, I really don't want to go, Drew.'

'Oh yeah? So I have to go by myself do I? I just hope some gorgeous girl takes pity on me, then,' Drew joked. 'Sure you won't change your mind?'

Clearly, if she wouldn't go to Anticipation with Drew, then he wouldn't see her at all. Right now Carole felt she couldn't deal with another upsetting event. She could stick to her point of view and spend the exam period wondering whether Drew had dropped her, or she could grit her teeth and get through the evening. It didn't seem like much of a choice.

'All right,' she said. 'Maybe it would cheer me up to have a night out.'

But next morning the old woman from the flat

downstairs came to their door with a postcard which had been delivered to her by mistake. Carole's heart leapt at the sight of the American postmark. It was a relief to know her dad hadn't forgotten her, and then it was depressing to find that the postcard itself was little more than a list of the places he'd seen.

No loving words—no special comments. Only a brief 'Hope your exams go well' at the end, which meant he didn't plan to write again until after her exams. Carole tried to tell herself she didn't care, but her heart felt like a block of ice wedged into her chest.

Somehow, even among the familiar sights and sounds of Anticipation, she couldn't manage to get into the party spirit. Finally she excused herself and headed for the toilets, hoping to pull herself together. Near the door, she paused to ease a contact lens away from her aching eye. Next minute it popped out on the floor.

'Oh no!' Carole wailed. 'That's all I need.'

She dropped onto her hands and knees and began to crawl about, patting the ground carefully and sniffing as she went. People kept hurrying past, laughing and joking, but no one stopped to help and she couldn't get the words out to ask them. Carole was getting desperate when someone appeared at her side.

'Contact lens trouble?' Larry asked, and she nodded miserably. 'Thought so. I've got contact lenses too, and you wouldn't believe the places I've dropped them in my time. Never mind, I've put a tape on, so I needn't go back for a bit, and I've got the torch I use for locating the records. We'll find your lens in no time, Caro.'

He moved the torch beam systematically this way and that and, sure enough, the piece of plastic soon winked at them from a crack in the floor. Carole snatched it up in relief.

'Thanks, Larry,' she said and burst into tears.

He put his arm around her and patted her shoulder for a while. 'Hey hey,' he said at last. 'No one turns on the waterworks like that over a contact lens. What's the real story?'

Without stopping to think, Carole let it all pour out. Her dad, the earrings, Christmas dinner, Drew, the exams—everything. It was a comfort to lean against Larry's shoulder and feel there was someone listening to her.

'No doubt about it, you're in a mess,' Larry said when she finished, and somehow that was comforting too. At least he wasn't telling her everything was okay, when she knew it wasn't.

'Yeah, it's a mess and I'm stuck in it,' she answered, feeling sorry for herself.

'Hmm. I'm not so sure about that. My mum always said, "You can't break the bundle, but sometimes you can break the sticks, one at a time." Let's look at the sticks in your bundle. I reckon the exams are your biggest stick. You won't feel too good about yourself if you look back on this time in the knowledge that you blew it. And the best way to pass your exams is to go in feeling rested and confident.'

'I know that,' Carole snapped, feeling the panic rise in her again. 'But I have to get those earrings made.'

'One thing at a time,' Larry reminded her. 'You need to rest, so you need to put aside the earrings until after the exams. On the other hand, you want to meet your quota of earrings—so maybe you need to let your friends help you, after all. It'd solve a lot of your problems if you worked on the earrings after the exams at the Corellis'—like they suggested in the first place.'

Carole wanted to object but she was too exhausted to argue. Besides, what Larry was saying made a lot of sense. Okay, she'd wanted to be independent, except that she'd taken on too much. The Corellis wanted to help. Why shouldn't she let them?

'It all seems pretty simple, when you put it like that,' she said in surprise. 'Thanks, Larry. I feel heaps better.'

'No sweat.' Larry hesitated, pushing at his red curls. 'There's just one more thing, Caro. Have a think about the way you feel about Christmas. I mean, you're talking as though everyone but you will be part of a large family gathering on Christmas Day, and it's not true. Take me, for example, I'm an only child and both my parents are dead. That's not a great start for a large family gathering, right?'

'Oh, I'm really sorry,' Carole exclaimed, but Larry shook his head.

'Don't be. I get by. I know there's a lot of

hype about Christmas being a family time—on Christmas cards, in the ads, in movies and stories—but Caro, we can all make up our minds about how much notice we take of that. You can either knock yourself out, trying to create the perfect Christmas, or you can try to work out what suits you.'

'Well it suits me to try to create the perfect Christmas,' Carole said stubbornly and Larry laughed.

'Fair enough. I'd better get back to my job now, but I'll see you round, Caro.'

Carole drifted off to clean her contact lens and fit it in. Normally she would've had the beginnings of a headache from looking at the world one-eyed, but at the moment her brain felt crystal clear.

Larry had solved all her problems. Larry had given her a nickname. Larry was the most wonderful man on earth, and she had the feeling he really liked her, too. Why else would he go out of his way to be nice to her all the time?

When she returned to the dance floor to find Drew whirling around with a stunning girl in black, Carole just smiled to herself. Drew was so immature sometimes, not like Larry. And when Drew left the girl at the end of the track and came sauntering over, Carole didn't even bother to congratulate herself on being cooler than him for once.

She was too busy thinking about the way Larry had put his arm around her. For once she'd been hugged by someone who was much taller than her. For once she'd come across a shoulder she could lean on.

Chapter 10

The exams were a breeze. To anyone else, Carole might've seemed to be working hard, but now that she'd put the earrings aside for the moment, she felt like she was practically on holiday. Though she didn't always confess it to her friends, she enjoyed her schoolwork and revision was no big hassle. There were a few bad moments during the actual exams, when she wondered whether she knew enough about her particular questions, but on the whole she felt she hadn't done too badly.

However, doing okay in the exams didn't leave her any richer than before. With every phone call, Drew's plans for celebrating the end of exams got wilder and wilder. Carole doubted whether she could've afforded them if the hundred dollars had remained untouched, but with twenty dollars left, she was definitely a non-starter.

So how come she was still going along with

Drew? Sometimes Carole wondered whether she was being chicken. Other times she wondered whether she still believed in fairytales—did she hope she'd wake up on the morning after the exams and find her shoes stuffed full of hundred dollar notes and a letter saying, 'Cinderella, you *shall* go to the ball'?

Basically, though, she knew it'd be wrong to fight with Drew in the middle of their exams, especially when it was something she should've brought up long before. She remembered Larry's advice about breaking the sticks one by one, instead of trying to break the whole bundle, and she felt sure it was better to be patient. With luck, she might think of some brilliant solution that would settle everything.

Carole's exams finished a day earlier than most of her friends. Mish was out for the morning, so she decided to have her own private celebration by making a start on the remaining holly earrings. She was twisting the warm plastic into shape when she heard footsteps which stopped outside the door. Hastily she hid the tray of leaves in her bedroom and went to answer the knock.

She was about to jokingly accuse Mish of forgetting her keys again when she realised she was face to face with Drew. 'Oh, hi,' Carole said in surprise. 'I didn't expect to see you here.'

'No, you wouldn't have,' Drew said, looking pleased. 'As soon as my exam was over, I rang a cab and came straight here. A few of us are going to lunch at Venezio's restaurant to celebrate, so I thought I'd collect you and take you along.'

'Did you think about ringing me first, to ask my opinion?' Carole said coldly.

Drew looked a bit taken aback but then he recovered. 'Sorry, I know that would've given you time to change, except it would've wrecked my surprise as well. Don't worry, the taxi can wait just as long as you want it to. This is a special day—the first day of freedom. We can afford to splash our money around a bit.'

'Maybe you'd like to burn a few fifty dollar notes in the ashtray while you're waiting,' Carole suggested angrily. 'Honestly, Drew, you're totally out of touch with real life. It's like you think it's impossible to be happy without all these expensive props. Some kids'll be eating fish and chips in the park after their exams, and I bet they'll enjoy themselves just as much as you will at Venezio's.'

Drew raised an eyebrow. 'I'm sure they will. The reason for going to Venezio's is that our friends will be there—or doesn't that mean anything to you all of a sudden, Carole?'

'No, the thing that's changed is that all of a sudden I can't afford the entry fee. Some of my friends won't mind, of course. I know that already, from the Corellis. But I'm sure I'll lose a few friends, now I have to admit I can't toss money round like it was going out of style, not any more. What about you, Drew? Will you be one of the friends I lose, or not?'

'You've lost me already, Carole, I can tell you that. I don't know what you're on about. I came here specially to make sure you could have some fun after the exams, and instead of being pleased, you just shout all this stuff at me I can't understand. What's going on? Are you trying to give me the push, or something?'

'I'm trying to make you understand,' Carole said, her cheeks going bright red. 'I know it's coming out wrong but, like you said, you took me by surprise. I never expected to have to sort all this out in the middle of the afternoon, with a taxi waiting!'

'Sort *what* out?' Drew yelled. 'There's nothing to sort out, as far as I'm aware. If the taxi bothers you, then either you go and get changed or you tell me to go to Venezio's on my own. I'm easy either way, so just make up your mind.'

'Oh wow!' Carole rolled her eyes up to the ceiling. 'You don't even know what I'm talking about, do you? What do I need to say to get through to you? Here!' She grabbed her purse and tipped it upside down. Two twenty cent coins dropped out and a twenty dollar note floated after them. 'That's all the money I've got. I can't afford to go to Venezio's, Drew. Got that? I can't afford it.'

'Well that's nothing to get worked up about,' Drew said, backing away. 'I can lend you the money easily. Come on and — '

'Did you hear me? I said, that's all the money I've got. I couldn't pay you back unless — '

'I think I'm starting to get the point at last,' Drew interrupted in his turn. 'It's not like you to carry on about money like this, Carole. There's obviously something more behind it—and I think you might've had the guts to tell me straight out you were trying to get rid of me. If that's the way you feel, I'll go. But I won't be coming back.'

There was another knock on the screen door and Carole realised that the taxi driver had been standing there for a while. 'You ready now, or do you want to finish the fight first?' he asked with interest.

'I'm not fighting with him,' Carole said with dignity. 'He's not worth it.'

'Good on you, love,' the driver grinned. 'You tell him. I reckon I'll wait down in the cab.'

As he turned to go, Drew pushed the wire door. 'I suppose I'd better go too,' he said bitterly. 'Otherwise you'll only get even more upset about the fact that I'm wasting money, since money's suddenly becoming so important to you.'

'It's important to you, too, even if you don't realise it,' Carole said in a low voice. 'More important than I am.' Drew hesitated a moment, but when she added softly, 'Goodbye, Drew,' he turned and strode away.

Carole listened to the sound of his footsteps echoing into the distance. She waited for the tears to rise again, but unexpectedly she found herself laughing. Now that she'd actually told Drew what had been on her mind, she felt stronger, rather than weaker.

Even though it'd come out all wrong, and even though Drew hadn't really understood what she was saying, Carole felt relieved that she'd got it out in the open. And Drew hadn't even tried to sort things out.

With a heart-felt sigh of relief, she bounced over to the cassette player and put on one of her favourite tapes. Turning the volume up, she began to dance around the room, singing over and over, 'Good riddance, Drew. I don't need you.'

The knock on the door came as a shock. She hurried over, hoping Drew hadn't returned and overheard her song, but this time she found the old woman from downstairs on the doorstep.

'I'm sorry, dear,' she said timidly, 'but it's your music. I wondered if you'd mind turning it down a bit.'

'Oh wow. I'm the one who ought to be sorry,' Carole said apologetically. 'I do try to remember, Mrs Clarkson. It's just that … well, we've always lived in houses with big yards, and I keep forgetting how sound carries here.'

'You're much better than some of the young people who've lived here,' Mrs Clarkson assured her. 'We've had rock bands and all—I don't know how they fitted the equipment into those tiny rooms.'

Carole laughed. 'How long have you been here, then?'

'Six or seven years, I'm not quite sure which.

I moved here after my husband died. It was a shame to sell our old home, but both my children went to work in New Zealand and they don't get back very often, so it seemed wasteful, having all those rooms just for one person.'

'You must miss your kids. Have you thought about moving to New Zealand?'

'I'm not the adventurous type, unlike them,' Mrs Clarkson said with a smile. 'I've lived in this area all my life. My friends are here, I know all the people in the shops —I just can't imagine myself leaving. I suppose I get a bit down in the dumps around Christmas time, when everyone else seems to have their family around them—but I go to church in the morning and have a tin of plum pudding for lunch, and then in the afternoon I visit my friends, so that's all right,' she added hastily.

After the old woman left, Carole stood in the middle of the room for a while, thinking of Larry's words. Maybe he was right, maybe she was making too big a deal about Christmas. After all, plenty of people were worse off than she was—Larry with no family, Mrs Clarkson with a family who were far away.

If she hadn't decided on the perfect Christmas, then she'd still have most of her dad's money left, and she wouldn't have needed to have a showdown with Drew. For a moment Carole felt a twinge of regret. Then she told herself it was ridiculous. There was nothing wrong with wanting to give Mish a wonderful Christmas.

Larry had helped her a lot, but that didn't mean he was right all the time. Just most of the time.

No, if her decision had meant the end of her relationship with Drew, then that was just tough luck. She'd simply have to work harder to see that Christmas made it all worthwhile.

Carole was about to get her earrings out again when the door rattled for the fourth time. At last it really was Mish, her cheeks glowing and her arms full of parcels.

'Hello, darling. I hope you haven't had lunch, because I've bought a few treats. And I've got a surprise for you.'

After her earlier surprise, Carole looked slightly wary, but fortunately Mish didn't notice. She dumped her parcels on the table and went on talking excitedly.

'Since we moved in, I've applied for half a dozen office jobs I saw in the papers. I got interviews for two of them and one of them rang yesterday to offer me the position. But in between times I'd got talking to the woman who runs the local antique shop and she asked me whether I'd be interested in restoring furniture for her on a commission basis.'

'Hey, that's great. Which job are you going to take?'

'Well, the office job would probably pay better.' Mish paused and burst out, 'I like furniture restoring so much more, though, and I could set my own hours and—oh, Carole, I hope you won't mind, but I went down this morning and accepted her offer. We won't be living in luxury, but at least I felt I could lash out and get you a celebration lunch.'

'A celebration lunch,' Carole repeated weakly, and then she began to laugh. Mish stared at her for a moment, waiting for an explanation, but Carole didn't know where to begin.

'Post-exam fever,' Mish decided in the end, and she started to set out the cheese and avocados and crusty bread on their best plates.

Now that Mish had a job, Carole realised it'd be much easier for her to work on the earrings at home. All the same, she decided she'd still take Larry's advice and accept the Corellis' offer of help. For one thing, she had a fair amount of stuff left to make. For another thing, it'd be heaps more fun.

So she set herself up in a corner of the Corellis' lounge room. Mrs Corelli fed her snacks from time to time—Carole tried to protest at first, but Mrs Corelli was an expert on food, just like Gee was an expert on guys and Silvana was an expert on clothes. Since she'd decided that Carole ought to eat, she simply made sure it happened.

As a result, when Carole checked herself in the mirror to see whether she was looking pale and lovelorn since her bust-up with Drew, she found she actually looked better than she had for weeks. All the laughing and joking with Gee and Paul and Silvana had probably helped, too, because her face seemed much more relaxed.

'The truth of the matter is, my heart isn't

broken,' Carole said out loud to her reflection.

It was strange. Drew had been so important to her for ages, and yet she hardly missed him at all. In fact, it was almost a relief not to have to consider him all the time. When she went to Anticipation with Gee, she was able to hang around and chat with Larry in the breaks. The more she talked to him, the more she appreciated his wise approach to life.

'Honestly, I reckon it's true what they say about girls being more mature than guys,' she remarked to Gee on the way home. 'Drew and I hardly got onto any serious topics, but with Larry, I'm always discussing things that really matter.'

'Oh yeah?' said Gee with a grin. 'Watch it, kiddo. You'll be falling in love with him next.'

No, I won't, Carole thought to herself. I'm in love with him already.

Chapter 11

Now she'd realised how she felt about Larry, Carole's whole world seemed to change. Her work on the earrings became sheer bliss—she was happy to sit for hours, threading beads onto hooks and picturing Larry's face or replaying the last conversation she'd had with him.

Larry talked to lots of the people at Anticipation. He was always giving advice or sorting out people's problems. In a way, he was like a half-way house between their world and the adult world. He liked the same things they liked, he dressed the way they dressed, and yet he had the extra experience that made it easier for him to understand their parents' point of view and explain it to them.

Carole was sometimes tempted to feel jealous of the other kids who gathered round Larry, but she knew there was something special between them. Larry always looked up with a wave whenever she came in, and he had a warm smile that was just for her. Deep inside, Carole was sure he felt the same as she did.

Obviously, though, he didn't want to rush it, any more than she did. There was a gap in their ages, after all—not an important one, Carole told herself firmly, but still it was there. It was fair enough that Larry would want to make sure that her feelings were more than a schoolgirl crush, and she totally prepared to wait around until he was sure.

She'd never been so deeply in love before, and she wanted to enjoy every second of it. No wonder she hadn't felt broken-hearted about Drew. All the time, a far more important love had been unfolding inside her, just waiting for a casual word from Gee to make her aware of it.

Then another casual word from Gee sent her thoughts off in another direction. This time, Gee's words were, 'When are you going to start selling those earrings?'

Carole jumped guiltily. 'Oops, I've got so much into the swing of making them that I'd nearly forgotten why I was doing it. I booked a stall at the market, but to tell you the truth, I can't remember the date. I'll have to check my diary.'

'Well, the reason I asked is because there's a fair at the church next weekend. It's actually to raise money for the church, but I explained your situation to the organisers and they reckoned you could sell your stuff as well. They thought you were a good cause—and they thought your earrings might put people in a good mood for spending, too.'

Carole laughed. 'Okay, I'll give it a go. It'll be a handy practice run for the big markets.'

'I hoped you'd say yes.' Gee grinned. 'I've already arranged for Colin to come and pick up the earrings on Saturday. He's bringing some of his display stands from the shop, so you can set the stuff out properly.'

'Oh great, I hadn't thought about that.'

In fact, Carole hadn't really thought about anything but Larry since her exams had ended. It was time to get her money-raising plans into gear again. Luckily, Gee was keeping an eye on her. With her energy, she'd soon get things moving again.

'I d-don't know why you asked C-Colin to drive you,' Paul said irritably. 'I could've taken you in Dad's c-c-c-'

'Yeah, Dad's car would've been fine,' Gee said with a grin. 'Think about it, though. I just happen to be madly in love with Colin, which gives him an advantage over you.'

'Maybe,' Paul muttered darkly. 'If you c-call it an advantage. Personally, I pity the poor guy.'

'Never mind, you can drive us when we go to the market,' Carole said, and Paul looked pleased.

The practice run was a big success. Every woman who walked past the stall seemed to stop with a cry of delight and buy a pair of earrings for herself or a friend or a relative. Carole reckoned she must've taken care of half the Christmas presents in Gee's area.

'Mind you, there's not a lot of choice at the fair,' Gee warned her. 'You'll be up against some stiffer competition at the market. They sell all the latest gimmicks there.'

'I'll take my chance,' Carole said contentedly. 'At least I've recouped most of what I spent on materials. Anything after this will be pure profit.'

It was a relief to have money in her pockets again. 'You know, I didn't realise how important money is,' she told Mish seriously that evening. 'Of course I'm planning to get a terrific job and make our fortunes, but I'll never forget what it's like to be poor.'

Mish had brought home an old wooden box from the shop, and she was French polishing it at the table. She looked up with a smile.

'Yes, that's what Roger and I used to say.'

'But you and Dad were never poor, were you? I mean, Granny and Granpa live in that lovely house. And as for Dad ...'

'My mum and dad spent most of their lives paying off that house, missy, and they did it up with the money they got when Granpa retired. Okay, it's worth quite a lot now, since it's so close to the centre of the city, but they wouldn't want to sell it, so they're only rich on paper. While we were growing up, we were on a pretty tight budget.'

'Oh, I see. You had lots of brothers and sisters, though, whereas Dad's an only child. So he

have a few different lines,'she said. 'That way, people stand there for a while trying to decide between them. And with a bit of luck they'll end up buying all three kinds!'

Indeed, for the first half of the morning Carole was kept busy answering questions about how the holly leaves were made and giving the prices to all the people who somehow couldn't manage to see the neat price tags at the end of each rack. It seemed like hours before Paul came over to her with a cup of coffee and a bag of hot donuts.

'Go on, sit down and have a rest,' Gee ordered. 'I'm perfectly capable of handling the sales by myself for ten minutes.'

Carole sighed with relief as she sank into a canvas chair. 'Oh wow, I'm exhausted. How much money have we made so far, Paul?'

'Not a lot.' Paul opened the cash box and peered into it gloomily. 'In fact, not m-m-m-'

'Not much at all?' Carole looked scandalised. 'That's not possible, Paul. I've been taking money from people all morning.'

'Yes, but that's … ' He stuck on the next word and tried again. 'You've been t-taking three dollars for the tiny earrings, Carole. People l-look at the holly earrings, they ask the p-price—and then they buy the tiny earrings or mabye the s-s-s-'

'The sequin earrings.' Carole glanced at the racks and realised with surprise that what Paul was saying was true. The bottom rack, where the tiny earrings had been, was almost empty. And the rack of holly earrings was almost full.

'Damn!' Carole said furiously. 'What's happening? The holly earrings are the ones I was really counting on. Okay they cost more than the others, but more work went into them and they're a really original design. Can't people see that?'

'Yes, they c-can,' Paul said unexpectedly. 'No, h-h-honestly, Carole. I'm sitting up the back with the cash box. I can s-study the people who come to the stall. They p-pick up the holly earrings and they look at them really c-closely. They l-l-like them. But they don't b-buy them.'

Carole shook her head. 'I don't understand. It doesn't make sense.'

'We've got an incomplete hypothesis,' Paul said with authority. Carole stared at him in surprise, knowing that she'd probably stammer herself if she tried to say 'hypothesis', and Paul grinned back at her. 'That's s-scientific jargon, meaning that we don't have all the f-f-f-'

'All the facts?' Carole said. 'What other facts do we need? People don't like my earrings, and that's all there is to it.'

Paul shook his head. Jumping up, he loped around to the front of the stall and bent towards a young woman who was examining the holly earrings for the second time.

'Excuse me,' he said earnestly, 'But would you m-mind telling me why you're having so m-much trouble deciding about those earrings? Is there somthing wr-wr-?'

'Wrong with them?' said the young woman with a smile. (At least I'm not the only one who does that, Carole thought to herself. I wonder if Paul would like to finish his own sentences for once, though). 'No, they're wonderful earrings. It's just that—well they cost seven dollars and the holly earrings on the other stall are only four dollars fifty.'

'Wrong, silly Lou,' said the young woman with a smile. 'At least I think the only ones in the ... and Carole chanced to hear this. I wonder if Paul would like to finish his own phrase ... for once though? No, they're wonderful. There it must be ... well they're both lovely indeed and the only earring on the other half her one four dollars ...

Chapter 12

Carole, Gee and Paul stared at the young woman, open-mouthed. Gee was the first to recover her voice.

'Someone else is selling holly earrings?' she squeaked.

'Oh dear, didn't you know? They're mass-produced, of course, and yours are much better made—that's why I've had such trouble deciding between them. The trouble is that I'd only wear them for one day in the year, and with Christmas being such an expensive time ...'

'Hey, you don't need to ap-p- you don't need to say you're sorry,' Paul told her with a grin. 'We're glad to know what's g-going on. Here, C-Carole, you'd better run along and s-s-s ...'

Carole waited for a moment, determined to let Paul finish, but he flapped his hand at her and she ran along to see the the other earrings. It looks as though Paul doesn't expect to end his sentences, she thought as she went, trying to joke herself into a better mood. All the same, her heart sank when she caught sight of a green flash of holly leaves.

The woman had been right—these earrings clearly weren't hand-made. Where Carole's holly berries were small, iridescent red beads, these berries were blobs of red plastic. Where Carole's holly leaves were individually shaped, these leaves all clearly came from the same mould.

Nonetheless, although they weren't works of art, they were cheerful and brightly-coloured— and cheaper. Carole wasn't prepared to swear that, if she'd been shopping around at the market, she wouldn't have gone for price rather than design. After all, as the woman had said, you only wore Christmas earrings for one day in the year.

She trudged back to their stall, wincing at the sight of its colourful display. Gee and Paul were glaring at each other, as though she'd interrupted them in the middle of an argument.

'I sold our earrings to that girl for five dollars fifty,' Gee said defiantly. 'I know you won't make as much money, Carole, but it's what you'll have to do. I've written out some new price labels and—'

'Thanks a lot,' Carole cut in furiously. 'I'm glad to know I don't have to take any responsibility for my own life. I can just sit back and let you make all my decisions for me.'

'Sorry, I thought you appreciated our help, but obviously I was wrong. Do you want me to run after that girl and rip the earrings off her? Or shall I give you the extra dollar fifty myself, since it matters so much?'

'Look, I'm glad the girl got her earrings at cut price, because she was really useful to us. But I'm not dropping the price in general. I went to a lot of trouble deciding how much to charge for the earrings—you know that, Gee. If I'm supposed to change it all around, then I might as well forget this whole thing.'

'Don't be so stupid, Carole. At least this way you'll get some money. Maybe you'll have to settle for a slightly less than perfect Christmas, but so what? Most people's Christmases aren't perfect, anyway.'

'Well, mine's going to be, and you won't stop me, Gee!'

Paul had been dancing around them, flapping his hands and trying to interrupt, but his stammer meant that he couldn't get a word in. Finally, in frustration, he kicked at the leg of the next stall, shaking its display of wax candles.

'Oh-oh, the bad vibes are spreading fast,' a deep voice said. 'Come on, man, let it all hang out. Lay it on Tuck and Storm, and maybe we can help you work through the angry feelings.'

Both Carole and Gee were so startled they actually fell silent and stared at the small, round man, wide-eyed. He was worth staring at, with his bushy grey beard and long grey hair, his faded jeans covered in patches and his waistcoat embroidered with suns and moons.

'Are you T-Tuck or S-Storm?' Paul asked with interest.

'I'm Tuck, and this is my life partner, Storm.'

A dark haired woman, wearing a long Indian dress and a shawl dripping with fringes, finished selling a parcel of candles and turned to smile at them. 'You kids are probably too young to remember, but there was a time when everyone was changing their names to Rainbow and Sunshine and Sky,' she said in a soft, quick voice. 'I thought that was a bit boring, so I changed my name to Storm.'

'And she can really brew up a storm when she wants to,' Tuck said proudly. 'Saving the rain forests, protesting against nuclear power, marching for peace—you name it, Storm's been there in the front line. She's really in touch with her anger ... which is why I thought we might be able to help you.'

Carole looked away, embarrassed. This was getting a bit personal. In the hope of changing the subject, she said, 'Are you hippies or something?'

'Right on,' Storm said. 'The last of the hippies, that's us, spreading peace and love wherever we go. Like Tuck said, you looked as if you could use some of it.'

Carole and Gee bent their heads at the same moment and scuffed the ground. To Carole's annoyance, she heard Paul say, 'I r-reckon you're r-right.'

Hardly stammering at all, he outlined their disagreement. He's all right when he's repeating things other people have said, Carole thought as she watched him wander back to their stall to help a couple of customers. That's why he could say 'incomplete hypothesis'—because it comes from his university lectures. It's only when he tries to use his own words that he gets into trouble.

'Well, well, well,' Tuck was saying as she came out of her thoughts 'Christmas earrings, hey? There's your problem. You've been sucked into the commercialisation of Christmas where everyone's told you to spend, spend, spend—buying bigger and bigger presents for each other, spending less and less time together—shut up in isolated family units instead of dancing through the village streets together, bringing home the Yule log and sharing the wassail bowl.'

He finished with a grand gesture that almost sent a candle flying. 'What are Yule logs and wassail bowls?' Gee asked sweetly and Storm winked at her.

'Don't ask him,' she whispered. 'He doesn't know. But he's got a point, somewhere in there. Christmas used to be for the whole community, but now—well, think of the city during Christmas shopping. Everyone's tired and irritable, pushing past each other and treading on each other's toes—in the name of peace on earth and goodwill to all!'

Carole grinned at the picture, but Gee shrugged and said, 'Yeah, I know all that. I did a project on the meaning of Christmas in Year 8. Right now, though, we've got a whole stack of holly earrings on our hands. I thought you were going to help us decide about them.'

'No hassle,' Storm said promptly. 'You've got to let Carole do her own thing, and Carole's got to learn to go with the flow. In other words, split the difference and set the price at $ 5.99. I'll give you a bag of one cent pieces to use for change. Is that cool by you?'

Carole and Gee looked at each other and burst out laughing. 'That's cool,' said Carole. 'How much do we owe you for the change?'

'Just give me a pair of those holly earrings,' Storm said and Tuck looked at her in horror.

'Holly earrings?' he repeated in disbelief. 'That's a symbol of—'

'It's a symbol of three great kids who are trying to find themselves,' Storm cut in firmly. 'At least, that's what I'll think of when I wear them.'

Tuck considered for a moment. 'I can dig that,' he said finally. 'Hey, and when you change the price on those earrings, make it clear that they've been marked down from seven dollars. People like a bargain.'

Paul came over to say that he'd just sold the last of the tiny earrings, and Carole and Gee rushed back to their stall.

'For hippies, those two have got some good business ideas,' Gee remarked as she set up a large sign, showing the changed prices. 'They're weird, but they're kind of nice.'

'Some of their ideas are pretty strange,' Carole

grumbled. She'd had a strong reaction when Tuck talked about people buying expensive presents for each other instead of spending time together. It was as though he knew how she'd shut herself in her room, working to give Mish a great Christmas, but in the meantime leaving Mish to watch TV alone.

But Mish'll be pleased when she knows what I've done, Carole told herself. And honestly, she wouldn't have been any happier if I'd gone and watched TV with her. It's been a pretty miserable month or so, and I wouldn't have had anything cheerful to say.

All the same, she was glad to forget her thoughts and concentrate on the sudden rush of customers as closing time approached. The holly earrings were selling better now, and the sequin earrings were almost sold out. At least I haven't totally wasted my time, Carole thought with a sigh.

'How'd you go?' Storm called across as they were packing up.

'Okay,' Carole answered, 'except that there are still two hundred holly earrings that we never even took out of their boxes!'

'We'd better exchange phone numbers,' Tuck said. 'We go round a lot of different markets, so I could let you know if there are some places where they aren't selling those cheap earrings. You'd have a better chance then.'

'I suppose so,' Carole said wearily and Gee elbowed her in the ribs.

'Don't give up so easily,' she said. 'We'll sell those earrings yet, I promise you.'

'It's a p-p-p-' Paul began.

'Yeah, I know it's a pain,' Carole agreed, but Paul grinned at her.

'Actually I was going to say it's a p-pleasure,' he told her.

Chapter 13

Carole mooched around the house for the next few days, feeling pretty strange. On one hand, she was definitely depressed by her failure to sell all the holly earrings at the market. On the other hand, she only had to think of Larry and all her other worries seemed to vanish.

So, of course, she thought of Larry as much as possible. There was now a publicity photo of him in the foyer at Anticipation and Carole had pestered the guy in the office until he handed over a copy. Now, when her imagination failed her, she could always take the photo out and look at it.

It was unfortunate that she hadn't yet worked out a way to see Larry during the week. Carole had made some vague plans for going into the office at Anticipation one day and somehow— maybe she could offer to help with the filing —finding out Larry's home address. Then she could invent some errand that would take her into his neighbourhood, after that it'd be quite natural for her to drop in.

Somehow, though, Carole kept putting it off. She didn't doubt that Larry would be pleased to see her. It was just that—well, perhaps she was rushing things. And she didn't need to do that. She was perfectly happy to wait, holding her dreams in her heart and going over and over the conversations she had with Larry each weekend.

At least, now that the exams were over, she could go to Anticipation on Friday and Saturday nights. Gee wasn't always ready to go with her—to Carole's surprise, she was still going out with Colin from the bead shop and Colin wasn't crazy about discos, preferring to spend his evenings at plays or orchestral concerts. But Carole just smiled when Gee raved on about the things she would've considered daggy a few weeks before. She had plenty of other friends she could go to Anticipation with—Paul Corelli even offered to take her one night when Gee backed out at the last moment.

All the same, sometimes the gap between one weekend and the next seemed incredibly long. After her experience at the market, she found herself wishing she could ring Larry up straight away and ask for comfort. And for the first time she wondered whether all this waiting was such a good idea.

But then she glanced at Larry's photo again and felt totally reassured.

That Friday was another of the girls' nights out. When Carole rocked up to Anticipation with Gee and their friends, she felt like she was coming home. Surprisingly, though, her longing for Larry over the past week made her feel strangely shy.

Instead of racing over to say hello to him, as she usually did, Carole found herself giving him a quick wave and then heading for the dance floor. In the end it was Gee who took her by the hand during one of the breaks and dragged her over to talk to him.

'Listen, mate,' she said in her direct fashion, 'we've got a problem.'

Larry grinned at her. 'You know me, the original problem-solver. Tell me all about it.'

'Well, it's my problem, really,' Carole said, finding her voice. 'You know how I was going to sell my earrings at the market? Well, the two cheaper lines did fine, but this terrible thing happened with the holly ones.'

Larry was a great listener. His expressive face encouraged Carole to make the most of her story, so she could watch his anxiety as she described the way people liked her earrings but didn't buy them, then his horror when she told him about the mass-produced holly earrings.

'Oh no,' he groaned. 'Well, I suppose it proves you were onto a good idea, if someone else was prepared to make thousands of the rotten things. But what a shame, Caro! You think you're onto something new, and suddenly the place is so full

114

of holly everyone's got it coming out of their ears!'

He pulled a comical face and Carole had to laugh. 'Yeah, it was a bit of a blow,' she said, feeling better already. 'It's pretty expensive to hire the stalls, so I was hoping that I could sell most of the stuff in one hit. Gee and I were planning to take the left-overs around to the shops in our area, but I can't get rid of hundreds of earrings that way. Besides, shops take a big commission, and I'd end up doing heaps of work for not very much money.'

Larry looked thoughtful. 'Exactly how many earrings do you have left?' he asked

'Two hundred, plus I've got the materials to make another hundred or so.'

'And how much do you need to make on each pair?'

Carole hesitated. Her maths skills were good, but she'd never tried to do complex calculations in the middle of a crowded disco before. Smiling, Larry produced a notebook and they bent over it, working out the sums together.

'I can't promise anything, not yet,' he told her. 'But I think I've got an idea. Keep on with your work—and give me your phone number, so I can ring you if I've got good news.'

He touched her shoulder lightly and swung himself back onto the platform. Carole stood in a trance, unwilling to let go of the feeling of his presence at her side. I was right to wait, she thought. He wanted to ask me for my address when Gee or someone was around, so it didn't look like we were being secretive.

She sighed with delight, wondering what his next move would be, and then she jumped as Gee prodded her in the ribs.

'There, I knew Larry would fix everything for us,' she said, looking pleased. 'He's got a real soft spot for you, Carole, which is generous of him, considering how you resented him for replacing Mario. Personally, I—oh!'

Carole was indignantly trying to say that she'd never resented Larry, so it took her a second to work out why Gee was so surprised. Then she realised Colin was walking towards them.

'Hi, Giovanna,' he said, beaming. 'I decided I should give discos another try. So here I am.'

Carole waited for Gee to direct a freezing look at Colin. Her friend always got really mad when the guys she was seeing tried to step out of line—and she never let anyone but her parents call her Giovanna, either.

But for some reason Colin seemed to fall into a different category. Instead of glaring at him, Gee was all smiles.

'Okay, then I better make sure you have a really good time,' she told him promptly. 'That way, you might even give Carole and me a lift home in your car.'

'That was the general idea,' Colin agreed, smiling at Carole before Gee raced him off to the dance floor.

Well, well, Carole thought with a secret grin.

I didn't see Colin as being Gee's type—but Gee obviously has a different opinion.

She'd always wondered what kind of a guy would be able to get Gee to stay in love with him for more than a few weeks. Since Gee was such an expert on guys, Carole had always pictured her friend's ideal as being someone who was smarter and better-looking than the hunks she usually went out with. A pop singer, maybe, or a TV star.

Well, Colin wasn't exactly pin-up material. He seemed like a nice guy but you couldn't say his converation was incredibly witty. Gee had made a big point of telling her that he managed the bead shop, rather than just working in it, except that, either way, it wasn't the world's most exciting career.

No, there was no logic behind Gee's choice. Somehow, she and Colin had just clicked, and that was that. It's the same as me and Larry, Carole thought. We were drawn to each other from the start—that's probably why I reacted against him, because I was scared by the strength of my feelings, at a time when I was going out with Drew.

Drew seemed like a figure from her distant past by now. Carole had seen him at Anticipation once or twice, but he had always started laughing and joking loudly with his friends as soon as he noticed her. It was obvious he didn't want to be friends with her or anything, and fortunately he must've decided that it was better to move on to another disco scene, because Carole hadn't seen him around lately.

To her disappointment, Colin and Gee decided to leave early, which meant she missed out on the chance of a last word with Larry. But it didn't really matter. Larry had her phone number now. Larry had plans for her. She didn't even need to worry about the earrings and her Christmas surprise for Mish, because Larry had everything under control.

So Carole had no difficulty at all in waiting out the following week. In the mornings she worked hard on finishing her last batch of earrings, and in the afternoons she talked to Mish as they worked to turn the flat into a cosy home.

Then there were friends to visit and Christmas presents to plan. Sometimes Carole met old Mrs Clarkson on the stairs and talked to her for a while, and she was getting to know some of the other people in the flats as well. All in all, her life seemed pretty full. She hardly had enough time for all the things she wanted to do.

Still, she knew that things would've been really different without Larry in the background. Whenever she was down, she could always think of him, whereas beforehand she would've started thinking about Dad and Mish, making herself even more miserable.

Larry had changed all of that. And soon he'd ring and change her life even more.

Chapter 14

There was only one problem with having a good time—it cost money. Carole had learned from her experience with Drew. These days she spoke out frankly whenever any of her friends wanted her to do things she couldn't afford. To her relief, most of them respected this, and she had the comfort of knowing that they liked her for herself, not because of her dad's position in life.

All the same, whenever she went out, she parted with small amounts of money, for cups of coffee, a magazine, an icecream or whatever. If she saw something that seemed like a perfect Christmas present, it seemed silly to wait until she'd sold her last earring to buy it. And sometimes Carole simply forgot that she didn't have her dad to back her spending any more, which meant that once or twice she lashed out and bought things she didn't really need.

Gradually all the small amounts of money

added up to a large amount. Checking her budget carefully one day, Carole was alarmed to see that her savings had dropped below the minimum sum she needed to provide a Christmas dinner for Mish. She checked her addition carefully, to be sure that she hadn't made a mistake, but there was no doubt about it.

If Larry couldn't help her sell the holly earrings, then she would really be in trouble. Of course Carole still had absolute faith in him, but on the other hand he had warned her he couldn't promise anything. So she was really pleased when next morning, as she was working on the earrings, the phone rang.

Carole was so sure it'd be Larry that she took a while to understand what the woman was saying. 'I'm Ms Golding from Good As New,' she repeated in a louder voice, as if Carole was slightly deaf. 'I wanted to let you know as soon as possible that we've sold all your clothes, in case you wanted to use the money for your Christmas shopping.'

'Oh, right,' Carole mumbled, still slightly dazed.

Once Gee had made her suggestion about the earrings, she'd completely forgotten about Good As New. But after she'd put the phone down, she realised that Ms Golding couldn't have rung at a better time. Now she'd be able to get her savings back above the danger line, which meant she wouldn't be totally devastated if Larry had to tell her that his plans on her behalf had failed.

She went into the city that afternoon to collect her payment. When she bounced into the shop, Ms Golding looked up with a smile.

'I'm pleased to say we got a better price for your clothes than I anticipated,' she told Carole. 'Sometimes we have trouble selling the more unusual garments, and sometimes they go very quickly. I hope you'll be able to make good use of the money.'

Carole found herself telling the woman about her Christmas plans and Ms Golding listened with interest.

'Yes it is strange, isn't it?' she said thoughtfully. 'Christmas is supposed to be such a happy time, and yet for a lot of people it's probably the most miserable time of the year. I chose to be single and never regretted it—I've got lots of friends and generally I lead a busy social life. But when it comes to Christmas, of course, the family takes over—which can be a problem, if you don't happen to live in a family!'

'So what do you actually do on Christmas Day?' Carole asked.

'I'd like to say that I just stay home and read a good book,' Ms Golding said with a grin. 'But the truth is, I'm not strong-minded enough. I enjoy a quiet day on my own at other times, but not when everyone else in my street is gathering together around a Christmas dinner. So I generally meet up with some friends in the same position as myself, and we have a picnic or a barbecue or something we'll all enjoy.'

Carole gazed at her in surprise. 'That sounds more fun than staying at home and reading a book. Why would you want to do that, anyway?'

'Because I don't like to think I'm the sort of person who does things simply because everyone else is doing them,' Ms Golding said seriously. 'I'm afraid I'm not quite as independent as that, though. Once, I spent a year in Indonesia, so I was there during Ramadan, the big Muslim festival. Now Ramadan has no special meaning for me—and yet I found myself leaving the house and travelling twenty kilometres to visit the only non-Muslim people I knew, just so I wouldn't feel lonely and isolated.'

'I get your point.' Carole nodded. 'Christmas sort of puts pressure on people in a way, doesn't it? It's all about togetherness, but that makes you feel twice as lonely if you're not part of it.'

Ms Golding chuckled. 'Well, it's supposed to be about togetherness, anyhow. When I was growing up, we always had our biggest family fights on Christmas Day, because everyone was exhausted from the preparations. I actually enjoy my picnics and barbecues much more!'

Carole was still smiling as she walked out into the street. It was strange how, when she'd been feeling miserable, Ms Golding had seemed snappy and horrible. But now that Larry had changed Carole's world, Ms Golding seemed different, too. Carole would never have believed she could've had such a long and personal talk over the counter at Good As New. It seemed like anything was possible when you had a guy like Larry in your life.

She wandered around the city for a while and then decided to head back home. As she was walking up the steps at the flat, she heard someone running after her. When she glanced over her shoulder, she saw it was Larry.

Carole's heart missed a beat. She was so overwhelmed by the sight of Larry in her every-day surroundings that she just wanted to stand and gaze at him.

'That was lucky,' Larry gasped, still breathless from his run. 'I was out in my car, so I thought I'd come and give you the good news in person, but you weren't home. I left a note and I was just about to drive off when I saw you walking up from the station.'

'It must've been meant to happen,' Carole said, only half-joking. 'Hey, why are we standing around on the stairs? Come up to the flat and I'll give you a cuppa while you give me the great news.'

She shoved her hands in her pockets and kept her fingers crossed all the way to her front door, possessed by a superstitious fear that Larry would somehow vanish before she got there. But when she turned, he was still there, his red curls flopping over his forehead in the way that always made her long to reach out and gently push them back.

He stretched his long arm over her shoulder to

take the note from the door, but Carole got there before him.

'Hey that's my note,' she said with a grin. Wonderful as it was to have Larry there with her, she knew she'd still be glad to have a souvenir of his presence afterwards. Larry looked at her, a bit puzzled, so she smiled and said, 'Your autograph may make my fortune when you get to be rich and famous, you know.'

'I wouldn't count on it,' Larry said with a laugh, following her into the flat. 'As far as making your fortune goes, I think my present plan'll do better for you.'

'Oh yeah? So what is it?'

'Well the manager at Anticipation's been thinking about doing something special for Christmas. I had a talk with him and convinced him to give a pair of earrings to every girl who comes along on Christmas Eve. He's going to buy up your whole stock, Caro.'

Without even stopping to think, Carole flung her arms around him. She'd reacted instinctively, just as she might've done if Gee or Paul or Mish had brought her some good news. But instantly she was overwhelmingly aware that it was Larry she was holding.

All at once she was filled with a mixture of conflicting emotions. She wanted to bury her head in his shoulder and cling to him forever. She wanted to run and hide away from sheer embarrassment. For a moment she just stood there, feeling the wiry strength of his arms and breathing the smell of him, and then Larry gently moved her away.

'I'm glad you're pleased,' he said as he looked directly into her eyes, his hands still resting on her shoulders. 'Now we'd better get down to business. I have to make sure the price is okay with you, and find out when you can deliver the earrings.'

Carole made cups of coffee and sat down at the table, still in a daze. Things were moving really fast. Her financial problems were solved and, even more incredibly, Larry had held her in his arms. Maybe, before he went, he'd actually say something about the way things stood between them.

But, just as they were finishing the arrangements, Carole heard Mish's key turning in the lock. Hastily she swept up the sheets of paper on which she'd been jotting down prices and times.

'Remember, this is still a secret from Mish,' she whispered. 'I'll introduce you as a friend of mine, okay?'

Larry and Mish took to each other at once. When Mish went straight to the chopping board and began to prepare the evening meal, it turned out that Larry was also a keen cook. He and Mish started swapping recipes and reminiscing about the most spectacular meals they'd ever made.

'My favourite was a smoked salmon mousse decorated with red and black caviar.' Mish sighed. 'I don't suppose I'll be making it again for a while, though, now that I'm supporting Carole and myself on a part-time wage.'

Larry looked sympathetic. 'I was talking to a friend of mine who got divorced recently. She said she'd read a study which showed that women tended to be financially worse off after a divorce and men tended to be financially better off.'

'That's not what Roger's divorced friends used to say,' Mish remarked. 'They were always complaining about their divorce settlements, saying their ex-wives were living in luxury which they had to slave away to provide. That's why I decided I was going to be responsible for Carole and me.'

'Fair enough,' said Larry, 'as long as your husband paid for all the cooking, washing, house-cleaning and child-minding you undoubtedly did for him over the years. If he did, then you should have a reasonable amount of savings to back you in whatever you choose to do next.'

Mish giggled. 'Of course he didn't pay me. I did it for love.'

'My friend would get mad if she heard you say that,' Larry said, pulling a comical face. 'She reckons that when men enjoy their work, they expect to be well paid for it, but when women enjoy their work, they expect little or no pay. And she reckons that needs to change.'

'This friend of yours—is she just a friend?' Mish asked. 'You seem to have quite a personal interest in the subject.'

Carole caught her breath in sudden panic but

to her relief Larry said, 'Oh, I take all my friends' problems very seriously. It's just the way I am. And I don't see why men and women can't simply be friends, without any overtones.'

Larry could always be relied on to have unusual ideas, thought Carole. She considered for a moment and said, 'Yeah, I suppose it's possible. I mean up until now my best friends have always been girls, but I'm getting to be good mates with Paul Corelli.'

'Well, it doesn't always stop at friendship,' Larry said with a meaningful glance at her, and Carole felt a slow blush spread across her face. At any other time she would've been incredibly embarrassed by it, but now she felt she and Larry were getting to the stage when she didn't have to be ashamed of her feelings.

Larry left soon after that, and Carole was almost relieved to see him go. She had so much to think about she just wanted to to escape to her room and savour every second of that magical afternoon. However, Mish was roaming restlessly, looking as though she needed company.

'Carole, what did you think about that stuff Larry said?' she burst out finally. 'Do you reckon I'd be silly if I refused to take anything from Roger?'

'Well, Larry said that you'd done a lot for Dad, so it was only fair,' Carole told her. 'And Larry's usually right.'

'Actually I was asking for *your* opinion, not

Larry's,' Mish said with a grin. 'But that's okay,
I suppose it's basically my decision, anyway.'

Carole blinked vaguely. All the troubles between her mum and dad seemed very distant
right now, and she couldn't really focus on them.
She was too busy thinking about Larry.

would've been better off, wouldn't he?'

Mish bit her lip. 'Roger never talks about his childhood. I wonder if . . . oh, why shouldn't I tell you? You know that there are no grandparents on his side—well, that's because his mum and dad were killed in an accident when he was young. His uncle and aunt took him in out of a sense of duty, but he had a pretty hard life. That's why he was so keen to make a success of himself as quickly as possible.'

Thinking of her dad's past reminded Carole of Larry. Maybe his parents had died when he was really young, too. That would explain why he was always so ready to help kids in trouble. He understood what they were going through, because he'd been there himself.

'It was a struggle, but we really had fun in those early days,' Mish was saying. 'I was the receptionist and the delivery person and the ad writer, all rolled into one, not to mention talking through all the business strategies with Roger. Then, of course, when we became successful, our little firm was incorporated into a larger company. Roger got a job in management and I started restoring furniture.' She sighed. 'Still, I'm glad to know that you didn't notice any difference between your early life and your later life, Carole.'

She looked wistfully at Carole, as if she was expecting some particular kind of answer. Carole hastily banished Larry from her thoughts and said warmly, 'You've always been great to me,

Mish.'

Mish laughed. 'I hope I wasn't fishing for a compliment, but thanks anyway.'

Afterwards Carole found herself thinking back on the conversation. It was quite interesting to think of Mish and Dad building up a small business out of nothing. Maybe she'd end up running the earring empire of Australia.

She had her doubts, though. In fact, it was Gee who produced lengths of red and green material to display the earrings against. It was Gee who designed a huge sign saying EARRINGS FOR CHRISTMAS BELLES. (Although it was Paul who actually did the lettering.) In short, it was Gee who clearly had the business brain—and her dad was a designer of fine jewellery in the city, so either these abilities weren't passed down from your parents, or else Gee and Carole had been swapped at birth!

At any rate, as a result of Gee's eye for display and Carole's eye for jewellery making, their stall at the market definitely stood out from the others surrounding it. They attracted a lot of attention, too. Once again, every woman who walked past seemed drawn to the racks of glittering earrings. As well as the holly leaves, Carole had made drop earrings from huge red and green sequins, and since, with the Corelli's help she'd finished ahead of time, she'd also made some tiny earrings from the multi-faceted red and green beads she'd bought on sale from Colin's shop.

Gee had approved of the variety. 'It's good to

Chapter 15

Once she'd had time to think it through, Carole could see where she and Larry were headed. Larry had made the first move by coming to see her. Now it was up to her to make the second move, to show she was interested in him. And she knew exactly what to do.

In the meantime, there were heaps of other things to occupy her mind. First, Gee and Paul helped her to deliver the holly earrings to the Anticipation office. Carole was so excited by the cheque she received in return that Paul led her straight into a nearby newsagents to make a photocopy of it.

'You can sh-show that to your g-grandchildren,' he said with a grin. 'G-gran's first pay cheque.'

'And what a cheque,' Gee said, equally impressed. 'Oh, I know you worked for days and days to earn it, but still it looks so much better when you get it in a lump sum, instead of week by week.'

'The only trouble is that now I've got to spend it in a lump sum, instead of week by week.' Carole smiled. 'I've hardly dared buy any Christmas presents because I didn't know how much money I'd have. But now I can go on a real rampage.'

She spent the whole week fulfilling her dream by stocking up for Christmas as she'd never done before. Carole had wondered how she was going to hide her preparations from Mish, but then in one of her conversations with Mrs Clarkson, she'd had the idea of asking the old woman whether she could keep some things in her spare room.

Mrs Clarkson was delighted to share the secret, and she even worked out a plan in which Carole cooked the turkey in her oven and then carried it upstairs to surprise Mish. Carole was rapt in the idea and it seemed to her that everything in her life was working out at last.

So, when she walked into Anticipation on Christmas Eve, she felt like she was walking on air. It gave her a real buzz to see holly earrings bobbing all around her and to know she'd made them. Suddenly the world didn't seem as scary as it had when she first moved into the flat. Okay, she didn't have the cushioning effect of her dad's money any more, but she'd begun to learn how to make her own way.

She raced around saying hi to her friends and receiving compliments on her earrings from those in the know. Then, to Carole's alarm she spotted Drew ahead of her in the crowd. There were so many people at Anticipation that it was hard to get away, and before Carole could wriggle through a near-by gap, Drew had come over to her.

'Listen, Carole, I've wanted to talk to you for ages,' he said earnestly. 'I know I was a total jerk before, and I don't expect you to forgive me or anything, but I had to tell you I was sorry. I don't want you to think money means everything to me. I know I must've given that impression, but honestly, I had no idea of what you've been going through, and at first I thought you were just trying to give me the flick. Then when it sank in, I didn't know how to tell you ...'

Now he'd started, Drew looked as if he was going to have just as much trouble knowing how to stop. Carole had the feeling that there was something important in what he was saying, but in her bubbly mood she just couldn't concentrate.

'Please, don't tell me all of this now, Drew,' she called above the music. 'Can't we get together and talk some other time—when I can hear you for example?'

'I thought we might get together tonight,' Drew said with a significant glance.

Carole laughed and said lightly, 'But you didn't expect me to forgive you. Surely that's a bit inconsistent.' Drew looked taken aback and she added, 'I *do* forgive you, though, and I *would* like to talk to you soon—just not tonight. Maybe we could have a dance later on, or something.'

She beamed up at him and moved on, leaving Drew staring after her. Wow, Carole thought in surprise, I sounded just like Gee. Maybe I'm becoming an expert on guys all of a sudden. Before this, she'd always tried to do what Drew wanted but now, without even trying, she found herself setting her own terms and leaving Drew to decide. It was a strange feeling, but Carole thought she could get used to it.

She hadn't gone much further when she caught sight of Gee herself, standing with Colin and Paul. Gee had to tell Carole in great detail how exciting it was to see everyone wearing her earrings, but after that they all headed for the dance floor. The whole disco was filled with a holiday sense of excitement, and Carole was glad of the chance to release some of her pent-up feelings by merging with the rhythm of the music.

Every time she danced with Paul she was surprised to remember what a good dancer he was, and every time she had to remind herself that he was a sports player as well as a brain, after all. On the dance floor he seemed so much more confident and sure of himself that he was like a different person. Carole found herself responding differently, too—at least, until she told herself firmly that this was just her good friend, Paul Corelli.

'I reckon I might end up totally dehydrated if I go on like this,' she said. 'I desperately need a tall glass of Coke, clinking with ice.'

'I'll s-see what I can do,' Paul said with a smile.

He tucked his arm around her and steered her through the crowd. Carole told herself that he was just holding onto her so that they wouldn't get separated, but by the time they were propped against the wall gratefully sipping their Cokes, Paul's arm was still around her waist.

Bending towards her, he said softly, 'Carole, you're very s-s-special to m-me.'

'You're very special to me, too, Paul,' Carole said brightly. 'Without friends like you and Gee, I don't know how I would've got through the past few months.'

'Th-thanks. But I think of you as more than a f-f-f-'

'More than a friend? Oh, Paul! Please don't say any more. I don't want to think about anything like that tonight.'

'F-fair enough. But it's taken me a long time to get my courage up. You don't have to give me an answer, but at least let me t-tell you I l-l-l-'

They stared at each other in mutual anguish, while Paul struggled with his stammer and Carole struggled with her desire to run away. Why did both Paul and Drew have to pick tonight to have their say—tonight, when she had different plans in mind?

As she stood there uncertainly, she realised that the music had stopped. Above the murmur of the crowd, she could hear Larry's voice saying, 'And I can see you all like those ace earrings, so I

133

thought you might like to take a look at the girl who made them—Caro Carmody.'

A spotlight swung in her direction and, as Carole blinked into its brightness, she could see Larry beckoning to her. With an apologetic glance at Paul, she ran towards the platform. Larry hoisted her up and presented her to the crowd, draping an arm lightly over her shoulders as everyone clapped.

Carole thought that she'd burst with happiness. The last of her shyness vanished among the applause and the lights and the music, and when Larry turned away to play another track, she stayed by his side.

'Listen, I know you've got no family to go to at Christmas,' she said. 'So I thought you might like to have Christmas dinner with Mish and me.'

'That's a lovely thought, and thank you very much,' Larry said. 'But I'm afraid I've made other plans. I may not have any family, but I do have a personal life apart from Anticipation, you know!'

His remarks were made jokingly, but to Carole they meant the sudden end to weeks of dreaming. She buried her face in her hands and burst into tears.

Larry looked up, startled. 'Caro! Caro, what's the matter?' As she sobbed on, he said with a different note in his voice, 'Caro, you didn't think that... that there was something more than friendship between us, did you?'

Carole nodded violently, too upset to speak. She could feel Larry drawing her gently into the shadows at the back of the platform, and for a moment she felt a renewed surge of hope, but then he went on, 'Please believe me, I never would've mislead you if I'd realised. With the difference in our ages, you see, I thought you looked on me as a kind of father figure, at a time when you were going through a rough patch with your own dad.'

'That's stupid,' Carole said through her tears. 'You're nothing like the same age as my dad. Besides you like me—I know you do.'

'Of course I like you, Carole. And I'm flattered to know I mean something to you. But I'm afraid it doesn't go any further than friendship on my side. I hope that, if you have a think about it, you'll decide that's enough.'

'But ...'

Carole stopped for a moment. Her dream castles seemed to have crumbled right down to their foundations by now. When she looked back, she could see that all of Larry's kindness towards her could easily have sprung from simple friendship. Even when she'd hugged him, that afternoon at the flat, it had remained a friendly hug, rather than turning into anything more passionate.

'But you said that friendship between a guy and girl needn't always stop at friendship,' she cried desperately.

Larry looked at her in surprise. 'Sure, but I was referring to your friendship with Paul Corelli. I've noticed the way he looks at you, and I'd be surprised if he didn't want to be something more than friends with you.'

Carole's last shred of hope slipped away from her. 'I've made a complete fool of myself,' she said miserably.

'No, you haven't!' Larry shook his head vehemently. 'You'd be making a fool of yourself if you decided to hate me for no reason. But love—that always gets you somewhere, even if it's not where you planned. Maybe this is all part of you becoming an adult and learning to stand on your own two feet. At any rate, let me tell you again that I take it as a great compliment. Okay, I don't return your feelings—but I certainly won't go home and laugh about it.'

Carole winced. It was painful to have her worst fears put into words, though she was glad Larry had said it. She would've liked to give him some equally honest reply, except she felt too numb to think.

'Now, why don't you just sit here for a bit and listen to the music, while I get on with being a DJ?' Larry said kindly, and she gave him a grateful nod. But, as the waves of sound washed over her, she realised that in fact she just wanted to get away and lick her wounds in peace. With a quick wave to Larry, she swung herself off the platform and melted into the crowd.

For some reason Carole was not surprised when, hesitating at the door, she found Paul Corelli at her elbow.

'Oh, good,' she said with relief. 'Could you tell

Gee I have to leave early, I've ... I've got a terrible headache.'

'Then l-let me drive you home,' Paul said promptly. 'D-don't worry, I know what headaches are like. I won't a-a-a-'

'You couldn't annoy me, whatever you said,' Carole answered. 'Thanks, Paul, that'd be wonderful.'

Paul was true to his word and they drove through the city in friendly silence. With Paul beside her, Carole was able to put off the moment when she had to think about what had happened with Larry. Instead, she just stared out at the lights which glittered in the night like the decorations on a Christmas tree.

I haven't lost all my dreams, she told herself. I'll just have to concentrate on Christmas Day.

By the time they pulled up outside the flats, Carole's numbness had changed to an unexpected sense of calm. She turned to thank Paul and found herself impulsively leaning over to kiss his cheek.

'Happy Christmas,' she said with a catch in her voice. 'See you soon.'

Then she jumped out of the car before Paul could reply and ran up the steps. Mish was already in bed, so Carole was able to go straight to her room. She got ready for bed and settled herself on the pillows, carefully keeping her mind blank. For five minutes she ran through her Christmas preparations, checking everything was in order, and then she willed herself to sleep.

But just as her eyelids were closing, a last tear slid slowly down her cheek.

Chapter 16

Strangely enough, Carole felt terrific when she woke up the next morning. She leapt out of bed, singing, and even before her contact lenses were in, the world seemed bright and clear.

Once she'd got things into focus, though, she suddenly remembered her talk with Larry. Immediately, Carole felt hideously embarrassed. How could she have got everything so wrong? What must Larry have thought of her?

Well, she knew the answer to that, because Larry had told her. He thought it was a compliment. Even though he wasn't in love with her, he still liked her—and he hadn't stopped liking her just because she'd made a mistake.

Actually, Carole could see how that worked. She had to admit she might've felt worse about herself if she hadn't had both Drew and Paul showing distinct signs of interest in her, just before she made a total fool of herself with Larry.

139

She wasn't in love with either guy but, no doubt about it, they'd given her ego a boost at a time when it needed one.

There was one difference between the two situations, however. She couldn't swear that her feelings towards Drew or Paul might not change. She had the distinct impression that she might've misjudged Drew, in which case they might begin to move back to where they'd been before. Then again, her friendly feelings towards Paul might be in the process of turning into something else.

Either way, Carole was prepared to wait and see. She was sick of making plans. After Christmas Day, she was just going to take things as they came.

One thing she *was* sure of, was that Larry's feelings towards her weren't likely to change. As she brushed her hair, Carole eyed herself sternly in the mirror and reminded herself not to start building up another set of dreams about him.

Larry liked her, and that was great. She could go back to Anticipation without feeling ashamed to look him in the eye. But first she had to state clearly that she'd created a whole fantasy around him. She only saw him when he was being a DJ and, as he'd pointed out, that was only one part of his life. Basically, she didn't know anything at all about the rest of him, and she was never likely to.

With a last sigh, Carole turned away from the mirror to face the new day. Christmas was on Monday that year, so the Christmas Eve celebrations at Anticipation had actually been a day early, which meant she now had the whole of Sunday to spend on wrapping presents and preparing Christmas dinner.

She wandered out to the kitchen, planning excuses for slipping down to Mrs Clarkson's flat. Mish looked up from her breakfast with a smile.

'Good news for you, Carole. Roger managed to get a cancellation on an earlier plane. He arrived back this morning and rang here first thing. He'd like to see you today, if it's possible.'

'Oh, right.' Carole hastily rearranged her timetable and said, 'I suppose that's okay. But I don't know why he's so keen all of a sudden, when he only wrote me one boring postcard in the whole time he was away.'

'Well, some people just aren't much good at writing letters. Give him a ring and see what he says.'

Her dad certainly sounded much warmer on the phone, and Carole began to feel more enthusiastic about the idea. Then, when she finally came face to face with him, all her resentment melted away and she flung herself into his open arms.

'I've missed you,' she gasped into his shoulder. 'I didn't know it at the time, but I've really missed you.'

'That's a pretty good description of how I've been feeling too,' said her dad, stepping back to get a good look at her. 'I suppose it takes time for all these big changes to hit home properly.'

'Could be. So how are you? How was America? What did you bring me?'

They raved away non-stop over lunch. Carole decided to keep the Larry episode to herself, but there were plenty of other things to talk about. She even decided to tell her dad about everything she'd gone through with the earrings.

'A very impressive outcome for your first business venture,' he said with a smile. 'I can see we'll be recruiting you for our marketing department any minute now... But I'm sorry you had to go through so much difficulty, Carole. I feel as though it was my fault for leaving you in the lurch.'

'I wasn't exactly rapt,' Carole said frankly. 'You'd always been there, and then suddenly you weren't. Still, I would've had to learn to make my own way in the world at some time. It was just a bit of a crash course. But honestly, even though there were some hairy moments, I got a real buzz out of selling the earrings, you know.'

'Yes, I can understand that. I think Mish and I were happiest when we were setting up our business, despite the fact that we had to live on the smell of an oily rag for the first few years. You should've seen Mish, dressed in overalls to deliver cartons from one side of the city to the other, then rushing over to answer the phone in her plummiest voice, so that the clients would think we could afford a highly-qualified receptionist.'

He smiled at the memory and Carole said

softly, 'So what went wrong?'

Her dad thought for a moment. 'Well, we merged with a larger firm. I suppose that these days they might've considered employing Mish as well, because her contribution and her ideas were certainly as great as mine, but back then women were a fairly invisible part of the workforce. I hoped Mish would continue to be involved by entertaining my business contacts, but to be realistic, that isn't exactly her scene.'

'You know, it's interesting,' Carole said. 'You both describe what happened in pretty much the same way.'

'Do we? You're lucky then. A lot of kids are faced with the problem of parents who are telling them different stories. Mind you, I'm not saying it was easy for me. After all, Mish walked out on me, and that always hurts. It was lucky that I was going away soon afterwards, so that I could get a bit of perspective on things—though I can see that it wasn't quite so lucky for you.'

'So how do you feel about Mish now?'

'I feel she was a part of my life that'll always be important to me, but I know that our paths have diverged to the point where we can't stay together. I'd been hoping she'd come around to my point of view in the end—and of course she was hoping the same thing about me. At least Mish left before we got to the stage where we really couldn't stand each other, and that'll make it a lot easier for me to go on seeing you. And seeing Mish doesn't want any financial assistance

143

from me, I suppose that leaves us with a clean break, in so far as that's possible.'

Carole hesitated and then said, 'I know Mish is determined to be independent, but don't you think you ought to try and convince her you owe her something?'

Her dad stiffened. 'What do you mean? I don't want to make a big deal out of it, but I have been supporting you and your mother for the last ten years. That adds up to quite a lot of money, you know.'

'Yeah, sure. You were just telling me about all the work Mish put into your business, which led to you getting your present job. Then there's all the work she's put into taking care of you and me. The wages for that would add up to quite a lot of money, too, I bet.'

'Hm. You really have done a crash course in financial matters, haven't you?' said her dad, eyeing her sharply. 'I have to admit there's something in what you say. I've always told Mish that she's too generous for her own good and it looks as though I was preparing to profit from it. All right, I'll consider all of that more closely. In the meantime, I notice you haven't told me anything about your love life. How's that going?'

Carole blushed. 'In a word, complicated.'

Even when she left Larry out it took the rest of lunch to explain properly about Paul and Drew. Her dad listened with his old interest, and as they drove back, Carole felt that they had managed to get things on a comfortable footing again.

144

No doubt there'd be difficulties in the future. Still, she was pleased with herself for having put in some of her own ideas about how things would go. (Well, they were Larry's ideas to begin with, but all ideas had to start somewhere.) From now on, Carole knew she wouldn't feel so much like a pingpong ball being batted to and fro by her parents. There were three equal players in this game, and she wasn't going to let them forget it.

Chapter 17

Carole's alarm woke her early on Christmas morning. She sat up straight away, feeling full of energy. She propped a hasty note for Mish on the kitchen table, and then went racing downstairs to Mrs Clarkson's flat.

The old woman was already bustling around, looking pink and cheerful. 'This is exciting,' she told Carole. 'I don't know how long it's been since I helped with a proper Christmas dinner.'

They plunged straight into a discussion of everything that needed to be done and, once the preparations were under way, Carole hurried back to the flat, to get out Mish's presents.

Her mum was already dressed and standing by the stove. As Carole came in, she quickly switched on the kitchen fan. 'I burnt some bacon,' she said guiltily. 'I hope it doesn't smell too terrible.'

Carole sniffed. 'No, actually it's quite a nice smell, but the fan blows it all away, anyhow. Well, do you want to see what's in these parcels?'

They spent an enjoyable hour, opening the presents they'd given each other and exclaiming over them. Since the Carmody family gatherings had always been small ones, they had invented a tradition whereby everybody had to guess the contents of each parcel before they opened it, which turned the whole process into an entertaining and sometimes hilarious game.

'You tricked me properly that time,' Mish said looking down at a box of chocolates which had been packaged to look like a book of carols.

'Carols from Carole—I couldn't resist it. Besides, you're usually so good at guessing. I thought it wouldn't hurt you to have a really hard one.'

They smiled at each other. An awkward silence followed, broken by Carole jumping up and saying brightly, 'Oh, I meant to give Mrs Clarkson her Christmas present. Do you mind if I take it to her now?'

'What a good idea,' Mish said over- enthusiastically. 'Why don't you have a little chat with her while you're there. She probably misses her kids a lot on Christmas day.'

Carole was puzzled by a sense of something false in Mish's manner, but she forgot about it as she rushed back to Mrs Clarkson's flat. They loaded a tray with salad, roast potatoes, cranberry sauce and a huge golden turkey, and Mrs Clarkson scuttled over to hold the door open.

'I've got the pudding on and I'll watch it carefully,' she whispered. 'Good luck with your surprise.'

Carole had left the door ajar, so she only had to nudge it open. She stood in the doorway, calling dramatically, 'It's Daughter Christmas.'

Mish's mouth dropped open in surprise. 'Oh, Carole! How sweet of you. But—but Mother Christmas has already been here!'

Carole looked down at the table. It was covered with bowls of salad and roast potatoes and cranberry sauce, and in the middle sat a huge golden turkey. The tray suddenly seemed very heavy in her hands and she bent to set it down carefully.

'You'd been so good, the way you weren't carrying on about whether we'd have a proper Christmas,' Mish was explaining. 'I thought you deserved a special treat. So I did some extra work at the shop and really splurged. There's a Christmas tree hidden in my bedroom—I haven't had time to get it out yet, and ...'

'There's a Christmas tree hidden in my bedroom, as well,' Carole interrupted. 'Well, I suppose it just goes to show that ...'

But before she could work out how to make the best of it, she'd covered her face with her hands and burst into tears.

Mish was at her side in a moment. 'Carole, Carole,' she murmured. 'We've both been so busy proving how well we can manage and how independent we can be, that we've forgotten how we used to consult each other. It could be worse, you know. We could have no turkey, but instead we've got ... '

'Two turkeys,' Carole said shakily. 'Well three turkeys, really, because I feel like a bit of a turkey myself.'

Mish giggled, and after a moment Carole found herself laughing, too. Mish gave her a sidelong look and reached for her camera. Carole nodded and ran to set up the card table. They brought out the two Christmas trees and prowled around the flat, choosing the best angle to display the double Christmas to the fullest advantage.

By the time the photo was taken, they were both weak with laughter. 'I'm aching too much to eat,' Carole wailed. 'Especially when I think of how much I've got to eat. Mish, is that a Christmas pudding on the stove?'

Mish nodded. 'And there's a cake hidden away as well. Did you ... ?'

'Yes I did. They're still down at Mrs Clarkson's.'

'Well, that's one thing we can do, for starters,' Mish said, suddenly serious. 'We can invite Mrs Clarkson up to help us with this food. If I hadn't been concentrating so hard on the family side of Christmas, I would've thought of it before.'

'I should've thought of it myself,' Carole said guiltily. 'I've been using her place for the last week, but—oh well, I'm only just starting to work out what I really want from Christmas. I'll do better next time.'

'As long as that doesn't mean four turkeys,' Mish said with another giggle. 'Listen, I know what we'll do. We'll invite everyone we know to come to an un-Christmas party tomorrow, and we'll serve them a fabulous buffet meal. People often have a feeling of anti-climax when Christmas is over, so we can use this situation to spread the good times around.'

'That's great,' Carole nodded. 'Otherwise we'll be living on plum pudding and turkey for the whole of next year!'

She hurried back to Mrs Clarkson's flat again. The old woman was delighted by the invitation, and Carole felt relieved that Mish had thought of asking her. She forgot to explain to Mrs Clarkson about what had happened, which meant that it was their neighbour's turn to be astonished by the sight of two Christmas dinners, side by side.

'Hey, and you can take a photo of Mish and me standing beside our own turkeys,' Mish exclaimed. 'Then we'll get a photo of you to send to your kids.'

'They'll never believe me, otherwise,' Mrs Clarkson said with a smile.

After all the turkey jokes, the dinner got off to a good start. Carole realised that it was nice to have Mrs Clarkson there, not only because it meant she wasn't eating a lonely dinner downstairs, but also because it took the pressure off Mish and her. On their own, they would've spent all their time trying to show each other how they were enjoying themselves. But now they were concentrating on entertaining Mrs Clarkson—which meant they enjoyed themselves without even thinking about it.

The dinners were a great success. They sampled slices from both the turkeys and pieces of both plum puddings and decided that everything was excellent. Mrs Clarkson returned to her flat, loaded down with packages of food, and Mish and Carole glanced at each other and then reached for the phone book.

So a wide variety of people moved in and out of the flat all of the following day. In their excited mood, Carole and Mish had egged each other on to invite everybody they could think of. There were people from Carole's school and business friends of the Carmodys ('Don't assume they'll side with Dad,' Carole had said. 'They may want to go on knowing both of you, if you give them the chance.') Mish's boss from the antique shop turned up, and so did Tuck and Storm with their three kids, whose names were Mary and John and Sue—they explained to Carole that they'd been christened Leaf and Tree and Flower, but they changed over as soon as they went to school.

The whole Corelli family came along together, except Gee who arrived arm-in-arm with Colin. Carole had invited Drew as well. ('Why shouldn't you ask both Drew and Paul?' Mish had said. 'After all, you like them both equally at present—don't you?') In fact, Carole had even rung Larry, but he was off to a friend's beach house, though he told her that he was looking forward to seeing her at Anticipation in the New Year.

Mrs Clarkson bustled about, pressing food on people as firmly as though she'd organised the party herself. All sorts of unlikely combinations of people were chatting away together—Carole noticed Tuck discussing rain forests with one of the business men, while Drew and Paul were describing the horrors of exams to Mish's boss, who turned out to be an ex-teacher.

'This was a fantastic idea,' Carole whispered to Mish in passing. 'Much better than my plans for Christmas.'

'Hey, we wouldn't have had all this food if you hadn't made plans for Christmas!' Mish joked in return.

But the best guest was still to arrive. Carole glanced up in the middle of a conversation with Drew to see her dad standing uncomfortably in the doorway. She raced over and hugged him with delight.

'Well, I thought that, if we were to manage all of this in a friendly fashion, we might as well start sooner, rather than later,' he murmured self-conciously, and Carole beamed at him.

He and Mish were fairly stiff with each other at first, and they seemed to have trouble deciding whether to stay at opposite ends of the flat or not. But the Corellis soon drew them into a discussion of life with teenage children, and after that both of Carole's parents relaxed considerably.

It's a start, Carole thought. Everything doesn't have to be perfect all the time. I know that now. In fact, I think I could quite get into—what did Storm call it?—'going with the flow.'

She glanced over at Paul and then at Drew. Paul caught her looking to him and raised his glass.

'I want to propose a t-toast,' he said. 'To Mish and C-C-C—'

'To Carole,' everyone chorused.

'Actually,' Paul told them with a grin, 'I was going to say, 'To Christmas C-Carole.'

Hi all you Dolly Fiction readers!

You've probably got heaps to say about the book you've just read — things you loved about it, things that could've been different, maybe — but you don't know who to write to, right? Well, if you've been hanging out to tell someone what you think of Dolly Fiction, or you just want to know more about the series, you can write to:

Belinda
Dolly Fiction
122–126 Ormond Road
Elwood Victoria 3184

We'd love to hear from you!

You just can't get enough!

DOLLY
FICTION
You just can't get enough!

Who Said Love was Easy?

When Jess meets Masami at her new school she doesn't even notice he's Japanese—she just thinks he's gorgeous! Masami shows Jess the art shed where she can work on her drawing, but seeing a prowler hanging around one afternoon really puts Jess off. Now she's learning self-defence and feeling heaps more confident, but she's still nervous when it comes to asking Masami how he feels about her. The fact that Masami's Asian seems irrelevant to Jess, but he's been so hurt by racism in the past that it just might be enough to keep them apart...

Publication date: December 1989

Christmas Carole

Carole's life is hard enough now her mum and dad have split up. It's even worse being short of money for the first time ever when she planned to surprise her mum with a proper Christmas and all the trimmings. And it's worse still when her boyfriend doesn't understand why she can't go out the way she used to and thinks she's trying to drop him. Larry, the new DJ at the local disco, really helps Carole with her problems and she finds herself falling in love. But does Larry really like her or is he just being kind?

Publication date: December 1989

Making Movies

When Annie auditions for a role in a film to be made in Spain over the summer holidays she thinks there's no way she'll get the part. But a few weeks later she's on her way to Spain. It's like a dream come true for Annie, especially when she meets Pascal, the Spanish guy who plays her boyfriend in the movie...

Publication date: January 1990

Everything Changes

Getting involved in the school production of *Grease* seems like a good way of escaping all the hassles at home—at least that's what Jo thinks when her best friend Nick convinces her that they should both try out for a part. Enter Shane Osbourne, the leading man in the production, and Jo realises that her problems are just beginning...

Publication date: January 1990

List of titles

1 The Look of Love
2 Broken Promises
3 Good Timing
4 My Type of Writer
5 Who do You Love?
6 I've got a Secret

7 In Too Deep
8 She's a Rebel
9 Stroke of Luck
10 Summer Escape
11 First Impressions
12 She's got the Beat

13 **Boys Next Door**
14 **You must Remember This**
15 **Designs on You**
16 **Is He for Real?**
17 **My Sister's Boyfriend**
18 **Hold on Tight**

19 **What's Wrong with Anna?**
20 **Country Blues**
21 **Making Headlines**
22 **Nobody's Perfect**
23 **Island Girls**
24 **Snapshots**

25 **Hungry for Love**
26 **Playing the Game**
27 **The Beat of Love**
28 **Tony's Choice**
29 **Change of Heart**
30 **California Girl**

31 **Who Said Love was Easy?**
32 **Christmas Carole**